COLL THE STORYTELLER'S
TALES OF
ENCHANTMENT

COLL THE STORYTELLER'S
TALES OF ENCHANTMENT

Lucy Coats

Illustrated by Anthony Lewis

Orion
Children's Books

First published in Great Britain in 2007
by Orion Children's Books
a division of the Orion Publishing Group Ltd
Orion House
5 Upper St Martin's Lane
London WC2H 9EA

A catalogue record for this book is available from the British Library
ISBN 978 1 84255 167 7
Printed in Great Britain by Butler and Tanner Ltd, Frome

www.orionbooks.co.uk

For Tabitha and Archie, my two unique and wonderful
Celtic children. A pháistí mo chroí – tá grá agam duit go
brách na breithe. L.C.

Thanks go to the team at Orion and to Anthony and Kathy Lewis
who all waited so patiently for this book, and to Rosemary Sandberg for her
unwavering support. Without Caitlín and John Matthews, I wouldn't have had
a clue how to pronounce all the Gaelic words (and I would have missed out on
hot hummus – yum!). Brue Richardson sent me to Wistman's Wood.
Inigo Vyvyan was my Cornish expert. My beloved mum, Prue Coats, found the
seeds of Skye stories in a dusty shop. My surgeon, Nick Birch, rebuilt my back
with immense skill. And lastly, my loving and long-suffering husband Richard
held my hand throughout the dark times, and gave me the space to let
Coll and Branwen's journey unfold.

For Isabella, Emilia and Rory.
Love, Daddy.
A.L.

Thank you to Kathryn for her technical wizardry that helped assemble this book
and to family and friends who entertained our three children whilst
we laboured over the pictures.

Contents

Branwen's Guide to Pronunciation and Places

> The stress falls on the syllable before the apostrophe

Alba – *now known as Scotland*
Aodh – *Ayd*
Armorica – *now known as Brittany*
Baobh – *Bave*
Bedwyr – *Bed'weer*
Caer Loyw – *Kire Loi*
Caoilte – *Keel'she*
Cathbad – *Kath'bod*
Cei – *Keye*
Cerridwen – *Ker-id'wen*
Cilgwri – *Kil-goo'ree*
Creidwy – *Kreyed'wee*
Critheanach – *Kree'an-ok*
Cuchulain – *Koo Hull'in*
Cuillin – *Kull'lin*
Culhwch – *Kil'hook*
Cwm Cawlwyd – *Koom (oo as in 'look')*
Cymru – *Kum'ree, now known as Wales*
Cynvael – *Kun'vile*

Dagda – *Dog'da*
Diarmuid – *Deer'med*
Drogh-Yantagh – *Drog Yant'ak*
Dunein – *now known as England*
Dun Fiadhairt – *Doon Fee'art*
Ealasaid – *Ell'a-sed*
Ellan Vannin – *now known as The Isle of Man*
Emain Macha – *Ew'in Mok'a*
Eochaid – *Yok'ee*
Eriu – *Air'a, now known as Ireland*
Fionais – *Fee'nish*
The Foawr – *Foo-er*
Gormshuil – *Gor'um-ooil*
Grainne – *Gron'ya*
Gronw Pebyr – *Gron'oo Peb'ir*
Gwion – *Gwee'on*
Kernow – *now known as Cornwall*
Laeg – *Loig*
Lugh – *Loo*
Lugnasadh – *Loo'nas-a*
Maelgwn – *Mael-gun*
Mochaid – *Mokh'a*
Nimue – *Nim'yoo'ay*
Oisin – *Osh'een*
Pwyll – *Poo'ihl*
Rhedynfre – *Hred-dun'vree*
Samhain – *Sow'in*
Sualtim – *Sool'tim*
Taliesin – *Tal-ee-ess'in*

Coll's Journey

On the Way to Uist
Stories 1 - 7

Stories from Skye
Stories 8 - 17

The Ellan Vannin Stories
Stories 18 - 23

Stories from Eriu
Stories 24 - 33

On the Way to Cymru
Stories 34 - 38

Stories of Armorica
Stories 39 - 41

Through Kernow
Stories 42 - 50

Coll the Bard Returns

In the Beginning

Long past long ago, behind the shadow mists of a thousand tales, the Islands of Britain floated on the edge of the world. They were lands of green hills and roaring seas, of soft sunshine and slanting grey rain, filled with magical oak groves and mysterious tall stones; where giants walked and fairies danced and seal-people sang amongst the waves. In those days enchantments lay in every clod of earth and grain of sand, and spirits of wind and water could be heard whispering in the sound of every breeze and ripple of every stream.

And in a certain hollow green hill, guarded by Merlin's spells, the Thirteen Treasures of Britain lay hidden . . .

The centuries rolled by, and invaders came from oversea. Cruel wars were fought, cutting through the threads that held the enchanted cloth of the lands together. Little by little even the strongest magic weakened and was driven underground. Only the druids and the bards remembered, passing on the secret knowledge and teaching the old stories in schools hidden in faraway places where no one would find them unless they were meant to.

And in a certain year, at the time when the sun was hot in the sky and the hazel nuts were ripening on the bushes, a baby boy named Coll and a raven chick called Branwen were blown by the winds to the island school at Callanish in Alba (which in these days we call Scotland). There they stayed for thirteen years.

The stars wheeled across the sky as a procession of druids wove its way around the tall stones in the Wintereve ceremony that welcomed the ending of the year. From the dark shadows behind the first fires of winter, the spirits of the otherworld chattered and swirled, each calling a faint warning through the mists that divided them from the mortal world.

Coll, now the youngest Bard, tripped over his robe for the third time that night. All evening there had been a buzzing in his ears that sounded almost like speech. He bit his thumb in annoyance, and suddenly the words came loud and clear.

As he heard them, his eyes rolled back in his head, his knees gave way under him, and he toppled to the ground, sending his raven, Branwen, flying into the night with a startled "Cark!" Then he began to chant the prophecy the spirits had sent him:

"Save now the Treasures all hidden.
Warriors fight in lands forbidden
and fire and danger ring the Merlin's nest.
Before next Wintereve has gone
Coll Hazel must find Avalon
And bring the Treasures to a safer rest."

Coll sneezed as he felt the hair of the best ceremonial bull's hide tickling his nose. He rolled over, opened his eyes and blinked up at the turf ceiling in surprise as he saw Ollach the Chief Druid, Fergal the Chief Healer, and Uath the Chief Bard sitting beside him.

"My head hurts," he groaned. "The spirits were very loud." Then he opened his eyes very wide. "Did I make a prophecy?"

Ollach laughed. "Coll Hazel," he said. "Always questions and questions, ever since the wind blew you here thirteen years ago, so small and so determined with a raven chick on your shoulder. Yes, you did make a prophecy – about the Treasures. And now I have a question for you. Did the spirits show you where the Treasures are?"

Coll gulped. Bards weren't supposed to forget anything the spirits told them, or they got beaten. He rubbed his bottom gingerly, remembering the words he had chanted by the winter fires. The Treasures . . . the Treasures were the thirteen magical objects guarded in Avalon by Merlin's spell. He closed his eyes, and at once the spirits put a magical picture into his mind.

"Avalon is a high hill with a spiral path," he whispered into the listening silence of his three teachers. "A green dome reflected in a lake of water as still as glass. I see an old man chanting a spell, and a boat coming through to meet . . . to meet me!" he finished in a strangled squeak. "That's where the Treasures are hidden, I'm sure of it. But where is it?"

4

"We don't know anymore," said Fergal. "Merlin's ancient lore tells us that Avalon is somewhere in the south, but it is a secret place which reveals itself only to those who need to know. And now the spirits have broken through the shadow veil from the Otherworld and laid a magical task on you to find Avalon and bring the Treasures here to safety."

"The sea raiders are coming again, and Merlin's spell weakens further at their approach," said Uath. "The prophecy you made tells you to bring the Treasures here, where the magic is stronger and they can be protected till the time is right for them to be used again. You must take a boat today, and sail south to start your search. By the time of the last moon of next autumn, you must have woken Merlin from his long sleep and found the hidden hill of Avalon. You must bring the Treasures here by next Wintereve, or they will be lost to us for ever."

5

"By my art I have seen that you will have help in unexpected places," said Ollach. "We have friends in the rest of Alba and the islands, and in Eriu, Cymru, Armorica and Dunein too. Visit them all, and use the help you will find. A bard is always welcome, and your stories will bring you food and drink and shelter. But first you must seek Donall Mhor. The druids at Dun Fiadhairt will know where he is. Now go. The tide is on the ebb, the winds are from the north, and your raven is waiting."

On the way to Uist

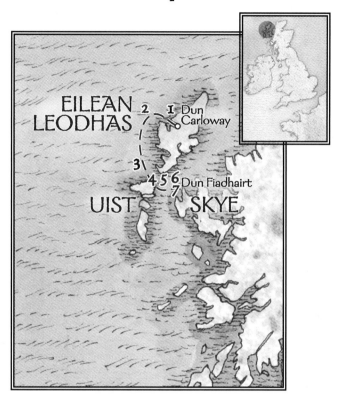

"I have no idea where to start," Coll said glumly, from the harbour of Dun Carloway.

"Let the stormwind of winter take us where he wills," said Branwen. As the sun set, Coll turned the nose of the little boat to the south, where the fierce north wind was guiding them.

"Tell me a story as we travel. A raven tale to put wings under us."

So Coll told the story of the Raven's Bride, and her stolen sons.

⊕ 1 ⊕

The Raven's Bride

"What should we wish for on such a fine, sunny day?" Ailsa, Mairi and Bellflower asked one to another as they washed their clothes in the burn.

"Why, a bonny husband!" they all laughed.

Just then an enormous raven landed on a boulder next to them.

"Cark! Will you marry me?" he cawed to Ailsa.

"What should I want with an ugly raven with hairs on his beak for a husband?" she said. And so the raven flew away.

The next day the girls were cleaning out the cowstalls when the raven landed on the pitchfork.

"Cark! Will you marry me?" he cawed to Mairi.

"What should I want with an old scaly claws for a husband?" she said. And so the raven flew away.

The next day the girls were tending the hives, when the raven landed in the apple tree. "Cark! Will you marry me?" he cawed to Bellflower.

And Bellflower said that she would, for she knew that ravens are magical creatures. So they were married, and in the day the raven became a handsome young man called Corven, and at night he became a raven again.

In due time they had a baby son, but the same night that he was born, a cloud of silver light came round his cradle, and soft sweet music sent the whole household to sleep. In the morning the baby was gone.

Bellflower ran around crying, but all Corven would say was that the boy had gone to the raven people, and that there was nothing to be done.

In nine months there was another baby, and again, he disappeared. Bellflower begged and wept, but still Corven would do nothing.

The third boy was born on a fine spring night, and Bellflower sat at his side, guarding him. But the silver light and the sweet music made her eyelids close, and by morning the boy had gone.

"This time you *must* do something," sobbed Bellflower. And Corven agreed.

"But mind you bring everything you own with you, or you will lose me too," he said.

As they set off in their fine carriage, Bellflower suddenly gasped.

"Oh, Corven! I have forgotten my little comb." As soon as she said the words, the carriage disappeared, Corven turned into a raven and flew off with a despairing "Cark", and Bellflower landed on the heather with a bump. Quickly she ran after her husband. But chase him as she might up hill and through glen she could not catch him.

As night fell she came to a turf hut where a red woman was spinning and humming to a sleeping boy child. "Give me shelter, in memory of my four lost ones," she said. And the woman agreed. Next morning Bellflower went on, and always Corven was just ahead of her. As night fell once more, she came to another hut where a blue woman was mending a kilt as she sang to a baby boy in a cradle. "Give me shelter, in memory of my four lost ones," she said. And the woman agreed. The third morning Bellflower went on, and still Corven was just ahead of her. But as the third night drew in, she reached another turf hut, where a green woman came to meet her, carrying an infant boy.

"I feel sorry for you, so I will tell you this," she said. "Corven will roost here tonight, and if you stay awake you can break the spell that is on him." So poor Bellflower sat on a hard chair and waited and waited and waited.

"I'm sooo tired," she yawned. And her eyelids began to droop. Just as they closed, Corven appeared.

"Oh wife, wife, what have you done?" he sighed. Bellflower woke with a start to see a single black feather drifting to the floor where a golden ring lay spinning in the silence.

"Oh, oh!" she cried to the green woman. "Where has he gone?"

"He has flown over the Hill of Poison," said the green woman, "and you will never get him back now unless you are dressed as a man and wearing horseshoes." So Bellflower put on a kilt, fixed some old horseshoes to her feet, and climbed the difficult climb up over the Hill of Poison and down into a crowd of men on the other side, who were all shouting.

"Whatever is the matter?" she asked in a deep, gruff voice.

"Oh, sir! The King of Ravens is come to marry the laird's daughter. He says that only a man with iron feet can cook the wedding soup, and there is no such man here!"

"I will cook the wedding soup," said Bellflower, showing them her horseshoe feet. So Bellflower cooked a tasty soup, and she secretly slipped the feather and the ring into Corven's bowl as it was served to him. As he took a sip, he brought up the ring and the feather in his beak, looked up and saw Bellflower and remembered everything.

"Fly with me, little wife," he cried, swooping into the air. Bellflower flung herself onto his back, and they flew off over the Hill of Poison, throwing the horseshoes behind them to prevent pursuit. On their way home they picked up their three lost sons from the green woman, the blue woman and the red woman, and I have heard that from then on Bellflower lived as happily ever after as anyone can who is married to a raven.

All was calm as the travellers passed Scarp and Taransay – until suddenly, a wrinkled grey body appeared by the boat, his ugly, whiskery face framed by huge yellow tusks. "Bull of the sea! You are far from home. Would you like a story of your brother on the land?" The great beast roared and turned to swim alongside them. "Then I shall tell you of the Waterbull who turned out to be a kelpie!"

⊕ 2 ⊕

The Elf Bull and the Water Horse

Long and long ago, there was a rich farmer called Macduff, who had many fine cows in his herd. One day there was a brawling and a squalling in the cowshed, and a great noise of bellowing. So he ran to find out what was happening, and it was this. A huge calf, black as a thundercloud, with nostrils redder than lightning, had just been born to his best cow, and it was he who was making all the fuss.

"Weell and a-weell," said Macduff, "there's a fairy bull must have been among the herd, for none of mine could produce a calf like this."

The calf drank the milk of three cows, and in seven years it had grown into a fearsome elf bull, which had to be penned by itself in a byre, chained with seven chains, for fear that it would do someone a mischief.

Meanwhile, Macduff's herd had grown bigger, and his niece, Ellan, had come to be dairymaid. As she was washing out the milk pails in the loch one morning, a stranger dressed in fine clothes came walking by.

"Comb my hair for me, dear lass, and you shall have a gold piece," he said. Now Ellan didn't much like the look of the stranger, but she didn't like to be rude, so she sat down with his head in her lap and began to comb his hair. It was boggety and tangly, and full of lumps of green weed, and soon Ellan realised that the stranger was none other than the dreadful water horse who lived in the loch, and ate unwary girls for breakfast. She didn't dare stop combing, but she began to hum a little lullaby that a wise woman had taught her, and sure enough, the water horse soon began to snore. She carefully untied the strings of her apron and slipped

out of it, leaving the water horse asleep. Then she ran as quick as a hare towards home. As she did so, there was a roaring neigh behind her, and the water horse gave chase, ugly and green and dripping with slime down all his four legs.

"What shall I do, what shall I do?" she panted to the wind.

And the wind breathed into her ear, "Free the elf bull." So she ran to the byre, and unchained the seven chains and the elf bull smashed his way out towards the loch, splintering the door to smithereens as he went. Fire came from his nostrils, and there was a terrible hissing and a steaming as he and the water horse crashed together. Weell and a-weell! There never was such a fight, either before or after. The two beasts spun and whirled all over the hills and glens until finally they crashed into the very loch where they had started and disappeared in a puff of green and red steam. And Ellan and farmer Macduff were never troubled by the fairy folk again.

After several rainy days at sea, dawn broke over the northern hills of Uist. A great sea spray had covered everything with a fine mist during the night, and Coll took out his harp to check the strings.

"Cark! What a terrible noise!" shrieked Branwen.

Coll grinned. "I see I shall have to tell you a story to soothe your poor raven ears while I tune it," he said, turning the wooden pegs as he spoke. "And what better tale than that of the King of Harpers himself?" And he began the story of Tam Linn and the Fairy Queen.

⊕ 3 ⊕

Tam Linn and The Fairy Queen

Tam Linn was the harper of all harpers. His fingers made music like jewelled raindrops, like moonbeams on water, like sunlight on young green leaves. And his singing – his singing was like all the birds of the air on a fresh May morning. When he played in the woods, the animals all gathered to listen, and when he played by the hearth, the girls flocked round like starlings on a roof-ridge. But the only girl Tam Linn had eyes for was Jennet, and in the velvet dark of a June evening, he asked her to marry him. "For you are the missing golden string on my harp," he said to her. And Jennet promised that she would marry him in seven nights, as soon as she had woven and sewn her bridal gown, whether her father agreed or not.

Tam Linn was so happy, he went into the woods to compose a new song in honour of his new bride. But he had clean forgotten that it was the seventh Midsummer's Eve, when the fairies open their mounds and ride abroad in the world. As he sang and played his harp, there was a faint jingling of bells and a thudding of hooves, and a golden mist moved through the woods towards him. When he had finished his song, he looked up, and there was a beautiful lady standing in front of him, dressed all in shimmering green lace, with pearls on her fingers and in her hair. Tam Linn swept a silver chord along his harp, and bowed.

"What may I do for you, my lady?" he asked.

"You may come and play at my Midsummer banquet for seven nights," she said, holding out her white hand. "For you are surely the best harper I ever heard."

"Is it far?" asked Tam Linn. "For I am to be married to Jennet in seven nights, and I don't want to be late."

"Not far at all," laughed the lady. "Just a little way along by the rowan grove, in fact." So Tam Linn got up on a white horse and rode by the beautiful lady through the rowan grove and down through grassy doors that opened into a green mound. Deep into the earth he rode, never looking back when the doors closed behind him. And that was the last that was heard of Tam Linn for seven long years.

Jennet grew pale and white with unhappiness when her harper did not appear on the night of their wedding. She laid her wedding gown in a chest, and went about her work in the house. But although many men asked to marry her, she told them all that she was promised to Tam Linn the harper.

"Nonsense," said her father at last, when the seventh year after Tam Linn's disappearance was approaching. "You will marry Donald the Blacksmith on Midsummer's Morning. He is a good man."

"He may be a good man," said Jennet. "But I shall marry none but Tam Linn."

"Obstinate girl!" shouted her father. "Obey me or you will be turned out of the house!" But Jennet turned and walked away, humming a tune that Tam Linn had made for her.

On Midsummer's Eve, Jennet got into her wedding gown and walked towards the river. All at once she heard a jingling of bells, and a thudding of hooves and she saw a golden mist coming down the road towards her. She knew at once that it was the Fairy Host, and she hid behind a bush till they had passed. But who should she see riding beside the Fairy Queen but her very own Tam Linn. Rage filled her heart, and she remembered what her old grandmother had taught her: "If you want something that belongs to the fairies, hold on till times seven changes, and it shall be yours." So she leapt out and dragged Tam Linn off his fairy horse and into her arms. The Fairy Queen screamed, her beautiful face changed to that of an angry beast, and she pointed her wand at Tam Linn.

"What I have I hold, girl," she croaked.

"But not if it was mine first," said Jennet firmly, clinging on as Tam Linn changed first to a slithering snake, then to a biting rat, then

to a pecking eagle, then to a clawing wildcat, then to a slippery salmon, then to a tearing boar and finally back into his own dear self. The Fairy Queen galloped away shrieking her defeat, with her host trailing behind.

"Jennet," said Tam Linn as he rubbed his eyes and kissed her, "where have I been?"

"A long way away, my dearest harper. But my gown is ready now, and we will be married in the morning," said Jennet, kissing him back.

In the harbour at Dun an Sticar, the children of Uist welcomed Coll. In return for porridge and a seat by the fire, Coll offered them a story . . .

"I shall tell you about a princess who lived out there, under the waves . . ."

And the children listened as Coll told of Diarmuid the healer, the magic cup, and the Princess Sea-born.

⊕ 4 ⊕

Diarmuid and the Princess of Undersea

Diarmuid was the son of Young Angus, the God of Love, and altogether a very magical person. As he was gathering red moss from the cliffs above the seashore near his home, he heard the shrill voices of the gulls calling as they wheeled and swooped their feathery patterns in the air below him.

"The Sea Princess is dying, dying. And you are the only one who can save her, save her."

Diarmuid didn't even stop to think. A patient needed him. He stuffed the moss into his pockets and dived straight into the waves beneath him. The seals showed the way, and soon he was at Sea-Born's bedside. She was pale and beautiful, and her green hair swayed and swirled in the water around her. Diarmuid put his hand on her forehead. It was cold as winter, but his magic was so strong that she opened her eyes.

"Fetch me the Cup of Healing," she whispered. "It is the only thing that will save me. But it is an impossible task, and I think I shall die before you complete it."

Now Diarmuid was not one to let a little thing like impossible stand in his way, so he set off to fetch it. After a long, hard journey he came to a wide silver river. There was no bridge and no ford and no boat, and Diarmuid wondered how he would ever get across.

"Would you be wanting some help, now, for a small reward?" said a squeaky voice by his ankle. He looked down, and there was a little brown man with a long beard.

"I would," said Diarmuid. "And what would you be wanting in return?"

"Only your friendship," said the little man.

"You may have that gladly," said Diarmuid. And right then and there, to Diarmuid's amazement, the little man picked him up and carried him across the river and up to the shining crystal castle on the other side.

"Thank you, my friend," said Diarmuid. But the little man was gone. Diarmuid banged on the door of the castle, which swung open at his touch.

"HAAAARRRHH!" growled a huge man in red armour, charging at him. Diarmuid drew his sword and fought for his life. Crash! Clash! Bang! At last the warrior lay dead on the floor at Diarmuid's feet, and he walked into the castle to find the Cup of Healing and take it back to Princess Sea-Born. Soon he was at the silver river again, and there was still no way across.

"Would you be wanting some help, now, for a small reward?" said a familiar voice by his ankle.

"I would, my friend," said Diarmiud to the little brown man. "And what would you be wanting this time?"

"Only that you take whatever advice I give you," said the little man. So Diarmuid agreed, and very quickly he was on the other side of the river again.

"And what is your advice?" he asked.

"Only this," said the little man. "That you refuse all reward from the Princess except a boat to carry you home." And Diarmuid said that he would.

After another long, hard journey, Diarmuid came to Princess Sea-Born's bedside just as she was taking her last breath. Quickly he took the red moss from his pocket and mixed it with some water in the Cup of Healing. Then he gently trickled it into her mouth. Her pale cheeks turned the colour of pinkest pearl, and she sat up, opened her ocean blue eyes and smiled.

"Truly, Diarmuid, you are the Prince of Healers, and I shall give you ropes of coral, and all the riches of the sea for your reward. And if you like, I shall marry you and give you the keys to my kingdom." But Diarmuid remembered the little man's advice, and said politely that all he wanted was a boat to take him home. Princess Sea-Born laughed and told him that he was a wise man.

"For only a boat of the Otherworld can take you there safely. Time runs differently here, and every second that you pass undersea is one of your mortal years. Without my magic boat to sail you home, you would be so old on your return that you would crumble into dust as soon as you stepped on the shore."

Diarmuid climbed into the boat, which was made from a large oyster shell. In the blink of an eyelid he was back on the cliffs where he had started from. The noisy seagulls were still wheeling and swooping their feathery patterns in the air beneath him, and for eyes that could see, the patterns read, "Goodbye, and sea blessings."

Waves crashed against the shore all over Uist, but Coll and the children were safe and warm.

"It is an honour to have a bard in the house," their grandfather said. "And a pleasure to hear your stories. Will you tell us one more before we cover the fire?"

Coll patted his stomach, now full of porridge. "Good hospitality deserves a good story. I shall tell you a tale of the Kings of the Western Isles from long ago," he said. Those kings had seven sons who captured a magnificent stallion on the shore. Of course, he turned out to be another kelpie . . .

⊕ 5 ⊕

The Kelpie

Seven Kings of the Western Isles there were, and they had seven sons, fine, bold young men to be kings after them. And on a bright morning, the seven princes took a boat and went fishing for mackerel. Not a thing did they catch, however hard they cast the nets.

But as they approached the Isle of Pigs, they saw a wonderful sight. A white stallion waited for them on the shore, pawing the sand and snorting clouds of white breath into the cold autumn air.

"Ohhhh!" breathed Prince Iain. "What a magnificent beast. Let us catch him." And all the princes agreed. But the stallion was none other than the dreadful Kelpie of Corrievreckan, and as soon as the princes had climbed onto his broad back, he whirled them away in a froth of spume and spray to his underwater kingdom. Only Donall, shield-bearer to Prince Iain, escaped to bring back the terrible news to the kings. Their grief and anger was dreadful to see. But for all their power on the land, they had not a drop of magic between them to bring their sons back.

Now it so happened that Prince Iain had a sister, known as the Jewel of the Isles for her beauty. One morning she was walking by the seashore, singing a lament for her lost brother and his friends, when a handsome young man walked up out of the sea.

"What a sad song for a lovely lady," he said. And Jewel agreed that it was.

"See," he said. "You have brought a tear to my cheek." And indeed there it was, shining like crystal in the sunlight. Jewel reached out a hand to brush it away, for the young man seemed so dark and lonely, rather like herself, and from the

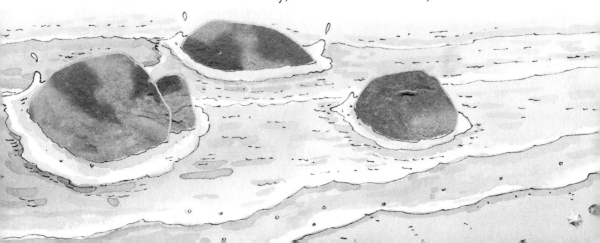

moment the tear touched her, she fell in love with him and he with her. They walked and talked until sunset, and then the young man kissed her and disappeared into the sea. Every day this happened, until one afternoon the young man fell asleep beside her. He looked so quiet and peaceful that Jewel did not like to wake him and so she sat there, humming and stroking his beautiful golden hair. But as the sun went down, her hand became sticky and slimy, and as she looked down, she saw that her love had turned into a pale horse, with a glowing white mane. She crept away quietly, for now she knew that the young man was none other than the terrible Kelpie who had carried off her brother and his friends. For seven days she avoided the beach, blocking her ears to the Kelpie's desperate cries, while she thought what to do. Then she went down to face him.

"Light of my life," cried the Kelpie. "Where have you been? See, I have been weeping for you!" And he pointed to the crystal tears falling from his sea-green eyes. This time, however, Jewel did not wipe them away. She knew his tricks now. "Will you not come and keep house for me in my palace?" he said. "For I adore you more than myself."

"If you love me truly, sea-horse," she said, "then give me my brother and his friends back." And because the Kelpie really did love her, he agreed.

"Look for them tomorrow night when this world and the Otherworld meet," he said, and then he galloped back to his palace under the waves.

"I will never love anyone but Jewel!" he wailed to his friend the Great Grey Seal. "However will I get another mortal maiden to keep house for me?"

Now, the Great Grey Seal was wise and clever, and he knew many things. He scratched his whiskers with a flipper.

"As I swam near the King of Uist's palace," he said, "I saw Jewel's cousin, Fionais. A pretty girl, but vain and cold and unkind to everyone including Jewel. If you can't love again then have a servant to keep house for you. Jewel's life will be much happier without her around." So the Kelpie dressed in his best green velvet suit, brushed his hair, hung fiery green emeralds in his ears and around his neck and swam up to the palace.

Music came through the doors and windows as he approached, and he heard a voice, shrill with cruel laughter. "What, marry you, Donall, a mere shield bearer? I have *much* better things planned. I shall marry a king at the very least." And through the doors into the Kelpie's arms came running Fionais. Her eyes went very round as she saw him. "Are *you* a king?" she asked.

"Of course," said the Kelpie. "And you shall dance with me all night, and be my bride in the morning." As he said this, he slipped a cunningly carved coral ring onto her little finger, and from that moment on she had to do just what he said, whether she wanted to or not. Jewel saw them dancing together, but every time she tried to get near to warn her cousin of the danger, the Kelpie whisked Fionais just out of reach. Soon it was midnight, and as the bells struck the hour, Jewel cried out and pointed to the sea. Seven wet and dripping figures were walking up out of the waves. All the young princes had come home and the Kelpie had kept his promise to her.

And when the rejoicing started, no one noticed as the Kelpie dragged Fionais down to his underwater palace, where he and the Great Grey Seal kept her busy polishing the coral for the next thousand years. As for Jewel, she married Donall the shield-bearer, and they lived happily on Uist until they died of a ripe old age.

The weather was still bad, but it was time to set sail again towards Vaternish Point and Skye. As the storm winds rose, the canvas flapped angrily. "Manannan of the waves save us," muttered Coll. Suddenly a glint of white and silver caught his eye. "Swans," he whispered. "Otherworld swans, linked by royal chains of silver. The sea god himself has heard me." As he spoke, the wind changed direction and started to die down.

"Magic indeed," croaked Branwen. "I feel it in my feathers. They are headed for Skye, the island of enchantments, as we are. Let us follow." So Coll set the tiller south-eastwards in the direction the swans had flown.

Branwen asked for a swan tale to honour them, and listened to Coll's story of the two swan lovers.

⊕ 6 ⊕

The Swan Lovers

I n the spring of the world, when the grass was new and mysteries lay behind every hill, there lived a young hunter named Aiodh. His arrows were made from the straight grey ash, bound with feathers from the wild grey goose, and the points were made of silver. There was not a man in the whole wide world who could shoot straighter or run faster than Aiodh.

One fine day he was coming home from the chase  when he heard the clear song of a missel thrush coming from behind a grove of quicken trees. He crept up with a hunter's stealth, and there he saw a beautiful girl, combing her hair by a black loch. She looked up and met his grey eyes with her own green ones, and in that moment they exchanged hearts for ever.

Ealasaid the Fair was her name and her mother was Morgei the Enchantress. Morgei did not approve of Ealasaid's love for her handsome hunter, and she was determined to put a stop to it.

"You sing like a bird," said Morgei to her daughter, "so a bird you shall be. But I shall take your song away from you and leave you dumb as a worm in the earth." And with that, she pointed her wand at Ealasaid and turned her into a swan.

Ealasaid climbed into the air with a mournful creak of wings and flew to the loch where she had first met Aiodh. She could hear him calling and calling her, and she flew silently round and round his head, brushing his cheeks with feathery white kisses for days on end. But Aiodh did not recognise her without her voice, and at last he drew his bow and shot her through the breast with one of his silver arrows. As she fell to the waters of the loch, she changed back into her own fair self and Aiodh ran to her, weeping. He cradled Ealasaid's head in his lap, as she sang one final song of eternal love to her hunter. The last note faded into the still air as she died, and Aiodh let out a great cry of grief.

"I shall never rest until I am with you again," he promised, as he carried her to the hill above the black loch where he had first met her and laid her down on the green grass. Food and drink turned to ash in his mouth, and all the world was grey for Aiodh in the days after Ealasaid died. He laid his bow and arrows aside and vowed never to kill another living thing.

Now Morgei too was in distress and despair at what had happened, for she had never meant for her daughter to die. So she went to find Aiodh as he sat beside Ealasaid's grave.

"No spell I can cast will bring Ealasaid back," she said. "But if you will agree to become as she was — a swan — I can promise that you will be together again for ever." So Aiodh agreed. And afterwards it was told that not one but two spirit swans flew from the black mirror waters of the loch to the enchanted land of Tir-na-nOg, linked heart to heart by a fine chain of silver. But such things are lost in the mists of long ago, and I cannot be sure of it.

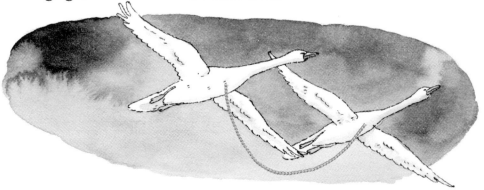

The swans were long gone as Coll steered carefully round the rocky tip of Skye and set sail down the western coastline.

"Rocks and rocks and more rocks," croaked Branwen. "I have never flown over so many rocks. Mind you don't sink the boat!"

Coll looked over his shoulder at her and laughed. "I've been sailing since you were a fledgling, Branwen. It'll take more than a few little rocks to sink me. Anyway, Uath taught me how these rocks got here. Do you want me to tell you?"

Coll told the story of the quarrelling giantesses who sought the secret of beauty.

⊕ 7 ⊕

The Giantess and the Secret of Beauty

The giantess Grein picked up her silver mirror and looked at her reflection as she lay on her back amongst the heather. "How beautiful I am," she sang to herself, stroking the softness of her black hair (long enough to make ropes for a thousand ships), and admiring her pale blue eyes (blue enough and big enough for the whole sky to drown in). Then she looked closer. What was that on the tip of her perfect nose? Was it one of the Cuillin mountains, resting in the wrong place? Was it a red-tipped volcano ready to erupt? No, it was . . . A SPOT! Grein jumped up and ran up and down the coast of Skye, her enormous feet making new lochs and bogs everywhere she trod. When she reached Torvaig, she stopped and cupped her hands around her mouth.

"Oh Fladday," she roared across to her friend, the giantess of Raasay. "Fladday, will you give me the recipe for your beauty ointment? For I have a terrible big spot on my nose that is spoiling my loveliness entirely."

Now Fladday was not beautiful. Oh no. She had hair like a hundred bristle brushes all on end, and teeth like mossy green tombstones, and a nose bigger than a whale's bottom. But before she had started using her beauty ointment she had been TEN TIMES WORSE!

She came out of her cave, rubbing her eyes and scratching her armpits.

"Spot?" she shouted. "Don't talk to me about spots. I've got a thousand spots bigger than your piddling little pimple." But Grein whined and whimpered and wheedled until Fladday was altogether fed up with her.

"Very well," she yelled. "You mix together the milk of a mother deer with some honey and three crushed silverweed roots and one other secret thing that you will just have to find out for yourself. Rub it on every hour, and your piffling pustule should disappear in no time." Grein filled a pot with all the ingredients. But she couldn't for the life of her think what the secret ingredient could be. She tried mussels and cockles, rocks and old socks, meat, peat, blood, mud, weeds, seeds and even her own pearly pink toenails. But nothing worked, and the spot was growing bigger by the minute. She began to get angry.

"Tell me the secret ingredient or I will throw such a big rock at you!" she bellowed at Fladday. But Fladday wouldn't.

So Grein picked up a small hill and hurled it across the island. *Splash!* it fell right into the sea, wetting Fladday's best dress. Well! Fladday wasn't going to stand for that. She plucked part of the cliff from below her feet and hurled it back. *Splosh! Splosh! Splosh! Splosh!* Back and forth went the rocks and boulders all day, until the whole sea around Skye was dotted and spotted with little rocky islands and both giantesses were tired out. And do you know, Fladday never did tell Grein the secret ingredient, and she had that big old spot on her nose for the rest of her days.

Stories from Skye

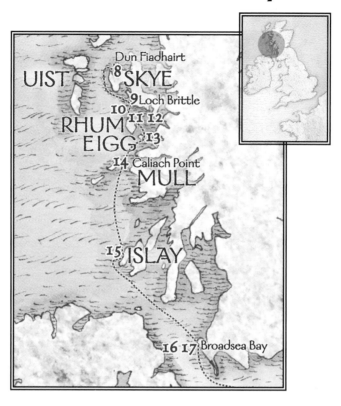

As darkness fell, the northern horizon shimmered with drifts of strange green light. Coll and Branwen landed at the end of Loch Dunvegan, where they could see two druids waiting for them.

The taller druid smiled. "Welcome to Skye, Coll Hazel," he said. "The stars told us you were coming, and look, the Blue Men are welcoming you to Dun Fiadhairt." He pointed up at the flickering lights over the Shiant Islands.

"Ah," said Coll. "I remember. The Nimble Dancers who came down from the sky."

"Come into the warm and tell us the story," said the shorter druid.

◎ 8 ◎

The Nimble Dancers

There were Great Ones of pure light who danced in the lands above the sky. Time did not pass for them, for there was no time. They had no fear, for there was nothing to fear. Distance did not matter to them, for there

was no distance – they could be wherever they wanted in the smallest flash of a thought. But one day Others appeared in their lands and began to dance too. Instead of pure light, they were made of something different, and as their dancing grew stronger, their whirling forms began to cover the pure white skirts of the Great Ones with patterns of colour. And then the Great Ones started to know fear.

"The Others must be thrown down below," they said. "Or we will all become as they are and disappear."

The battle lasted no time at all (for there was no time), but it was fierce and beautiful, and at the end of it the lands above the sky were empty and dark, for the Great Ones and the Others were now entangled for ever below, and the world beneath was a different place.

Torn mists of white landed on the green mounds of the earth and sank into the places beneath, changed for ever into the magical Fairy folk who dance and sing in the pure light of the full moon.

Tattered clouds of blue and grey and purple dissolved into the sea, changing into the dancing foam faces of the Blue Men who drag down boats to their caves under the stormy waves of the Minch.

And in the sky, ragged drifts of green rainbow lights flickered and swirled on the far horizon, as the Nimble Dancers searched the heavens for a road to take them home.

Coll and Branwen had sailed around the south-west coast of Skye to Loch Brittle. There they met Donall Mhor, who was sitting, looking out to sea, while a few fat white cattle grazed round him.

Coll told Donall that the druids of Dun Fiadhairt had sent him. "Have you ever seen or heard of a high green hill to the south?"

"No," said Donall Mhor slowly. "Though I once saw something of it in a dream. But there is a wizard on Manannan's Isle who has travelled further south than I did. His name is Broc. He may be able to help you."

Before they left, Donall Mhor asked Coll to admire his cattle, and then explained just how they came to be so fine . . .

9

Fairy Cattle

Deep in the sea caves of the King of the Sea-Folk there lived cattle as white as doves, as fat as butter, as gentle as mother's milk. And how did they get that way? Why, by eating the good sea grass of the Island of Skye. Every morning, just as the sun rose out of its sea bath, the fairy cattle were driven up out of the waves and into a secret pasture on the east of the island, and left to graze until sunset.

Now there was a man called MacDhonall who lived in the west of Skye, and he had a few scrawny cows which scraped a living out of the gorse and the thin grass around his hut. He had a wife too, and seven squalling children, whose bellies were never full. One winter's night the wife looked into the crock and let out a wail. "No more oatmeal, MacDhonall, not even enough for a mouse to eat! We shall all starve!"

MacDhonall sighed. "If I set out now, I can be at my cousin MacFeargall by morning," he said. "I am sure I can borrow a little oatmeal from him." He put his plaid around his shoulders and started on the long journey across the hills. It was raining, and he was cold, wet and miserable by the time the dawn broke. As he came to the eastern cliffs, he glanced down at the sea. And what a sight he saw! A herd of fat white cattle was just stepping out of the waves and onto the sand. MacDhonall dropped flat and listened as a high piping voice came out of the breakers below.

"The sand behind you
The land before you,
And never a speck of dead earth
Or a fleck of red earth between them
To keep you from your sea home."

Well! MacDhonall knew just what to do. He did not bother with getting the oatmeal. Oatmeal was for poor people, and he was going to be rich. Instead he took some earth from a nearby graveyard and gathered some fine red earth from a molehill and put them in his pocket. Then went back to the cliff, climbed down, and hid behind a bush to watch the fine, fat fairy cattle, rubbing his hands and snorting with laughter.

"Oh, how cross those sea-folk are going to be," he said.

As the sun began to sink, the same piping voice called out:

"The land behind you
The sand before you,
And never a fleck of red earth
Or a speck of dead earth between them
To keep you from your sea home."

As the cattle turned around, MacDhonall rose up and threw the earth he had gathered in front of them. Immediately it was as if a barrier had sprung up, and they could not move. There was a wail of rage from the sea. "Lost, lost, all my beautiful cattle lost! And to a mortal man too!" But MacDhonall was not listening. He was too busy herding his new cows home.

*The sun was just coming out, making a few late gorse flowers glow
like gold on the hills, as Coll and Branwen sailed south from Skye
to Rhum.*

*In Skye there grow golden flowers which are found nowhere
else. Their colour comes from the fairy smiths beneath the ground.
According to the story Coll told Branwen, anyway!*

◎ 10 ◎

The Fairy Smiths and the Golden Flowers

Deep under the mountains of Skye, deeper than
the sky is high, live the fairy smiths. Their forges
are lit by the fire of the earth dragon
who coils around the heart of the world,
and rivers of molten metals flow
through their caverns. There
they make necklaces as fine
as gossamer, dripping
with moonstones
and pearls;

43

spiral bracelets set with green gems and blue and red, rings for fingers and toes, eardrops like dew on a summer morning. And who is all this finery for? Why, the Fairy Queen and her ladies, of course.

Before every ball, before every party or picnic or indeed any occasion at all, the Fairy Queen and her court would fly down through the twisty, turny secret maze of passages and give their orders to the smiths.

"Emeralds and diamonds for the King's birthday parade!"

"Chalcedony and garnets for my nephew's coming of age!"

"Rubies and tourmaline for the Midsummer revels!" And so on, and so forth.

The smiths never grumbled, for they liked making beautiful things. But what they loved working with most of all was

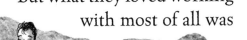

gold. They would scoop buckets full from their
rivers, and pour it back just for the pleasure
of watching it fall. And they would
heat it to such high temperatures
in the forge that it
melted beyond
melting and

rose up in a fine mist which
they caught on swathes of silk and
hung in their houses for curtains. But
every time they did this, which was often,
some of the gold mist escaped through cracks
and holes into the ceiling, and came out into the
upper world.

Just where the gold mist came out grew a patch
of dull green prickly bushes with dull drab flowers. Over
time the golden mist got into the roots of the bushes and
changed them, so that one late summer when they
bloomed, the flowers appeared bright gold-yellow against
the dull green prickles of the leaves. And that is why, if you
want fairy gold on Skye, you must ask the gorse bushes to
let you have some of theirs. You may get scratched if you do,
though.

As Coll landed on Rhum, he saw a girl setting a pail under a huge grey cow which was standing by a turf hut. She saw the harp on his back. Her eyes grew big and round. "Are you a real bard?" she asked.

Coll laughed. "Yes," he said, "I really am. And a hungry one too. Will you give me a drink of milk if I tell you a story?"

"I'd give a bard milk for nothing," she said. "But a story would be nice. Will it be one with a cow in it?"

Of course Coll knew a story with a cow in it – and much more besides – the tale of Finn MacCool and the mussel stew.

◎ 11 ◎

Finn MacCool and the Mussel Stew

In the long ago glorious days, there was a band of hunters called the Fianna, and at their head was Finn MacCool. There was a time when they came over from Eriu to the enchanted island of Skye, for the red deer ran in great herds on the hills there, and the hunting was good.

Every night the Fianna set their huge stewpot on two handy rocks by the western shore, and every night they filled their stomachs with good, hot venison stew. But there came a time when all the deer disappeared. Not even the best hunter among them could find a single trace of one — not a hair or a whisker.

Soon the stomachs of the Fianna were grumbling and rumbling, for all they had to live on was the milk of their magical cow, Grey Shoulders, who gave eleven gallons at each milking.

"What shall we do, Grey Shoulders?" asked Finn. "For although your milk is marvellous, we are big men, and we need stew to keep us strong."

Grey Shoulders swished her tail. "Mussels," she mooed. "Collect the mussels from the rocks, and stew them in my milk." She was a very wise cow in her way.

47

So all the Fianna who were not out looking for deer scrambled over the rocks, cursing as they scraped their hands and knees on the barnacles, and they collected the little blue-black shells and threw them into the stewpot with some milk from Grey Shoulders. It took a very long time to fill even the bottom of the pot, and meanwhile the Fianna were getting hungrier and hungrier and weaker and weaker.

Some of them even lay down on the ground, clutching their poor, empty stomachs. Suddenly, they heard an echoing shout from the direction of Loch Snizort.

"Deer! We've found the deer!" Strength miraculously returned to them, and they ran towards the voice, upsetting the stewpot as they went. All the carefully collected shells spilled down onto the rocks beneath, and there they stand to this very day, all spotty and stained with mussel stew.

The girl was called Elspeth. She was very pretty and the cheese was very good, so Coll lingered on Rhum, helping to milk the cow, and telling more stories about Finn. But on the seventh morning, Branwen pecked him awake.

"We'll never find that wizard Broc if you stay here," she grumbled. So Coll set sail southwards, and waved goodbye.

◎ 12 ◎

Finn and the Deerwife

Grainne was the daughter of a king, and the granddaughter of the Old Red Fairy, and she was the fairest woman ever to walk the earth of Alba. But her father had an enemy, the Grey Magician, and one day when Grainne was walking and singing to her beloved deer in the high hills, the Grey Magician wrapped her in a cunning mist spell and hid her away in his own palace in the Land of Cold Dark, where he tied her to a pillar and left her.

49

Now Finn MacCool was hunting near Grainne's home soon after, and as he followed his hounds, he came across a tiny old woman, all dressed in red.

"Help me, Finn," she said in a tiny old voice. "For Grainne my granddaughter has been stolen by the Grey Magician, and only you can rescue her."

Finn was not one to be refusing a challenge of that sort. "I'm your man, right enough," he said, and he set off at once. But the old woman called him back.

"Here are three things that you will need," she said, handing him a needle of green pine, and two pebbles, one clear and smooth as the moon and one dark and jagged as pain in the night. "Throw one at a time over your shoulder if you are ever in trouble." Then she floated away on a breath of the west wind, growing smaller and smaller until she was no bigger than a red spider speck.

Finn's journey to the Land of Cold Dark was long and lonely, and he grew faint and exhausted with the difficulty of it. But the animals and birds of the world helped him, and at last he was at the Grey Magician's castle. Rushing in with his sword ablaze, he cut Grainne's ropes, threw her over his shoulder and fled. The Grey Magician let out a bellow and leapt up from his feasting to chase them. Oh, how fast Finn ran then! Slowly the Grey Magician gained and gained, until Finn could feel his clammy grey breath reaching out to wrap them in its tentacles. Suddenly he remembered what Grainne's grandmother had given him. Still running, he fumbled in his sporran, found the pine needle, and threw it over his shoulder. At once a thick forest grew up behind them, and Finn and Grainne could hear the Grey Magician cursing as he cut his way through.

"That won't stop him for long," said Grainne. And indeed, soon the Grey Magician was closing in again. Finn took the white pebble out of his sporran and threw that. A shining silver loch appeared behind them, and again Finn and Grainne heard the Grey Magician cursing as he swam through it.

"That won't stop him for long," said Grainne. And indeed, soon the Grey Magician was after them again. So Finn took the black pebble out of his sporran and threw it. A huge range of jagged mountains reared out of the ground, and the Grey Magician roared with rage as he started to climb.

"That will hold him for a bit," said Grainne. "Just long enough for us to cross the Red River, and then we will be safe." But the Red River was so deep and so wide that they could not get across, and soon the Grey Magician's clutching fingertips were visible over the tops of the mountains. "I shall have to use my jewel," said Grainne. And out of her hair she took a round, red ruby which she threw on the water. "Bring me a boat," she commanded. Right then and there a small, round, red boat appeared on the water, and in next to no time Finn and Grainne were safe on the other side.

By now they were in love, and so they got married, and Finn took Grainne to live with the Fianna on Skye. Before she left her father's house, her grandmother took her aside. "Finn's presence protects you, but if he ever goes away, you must take care not to step outside the walls of your home. If you do, the Grey Magician will be waiting."

For a year and a day Finn and Grainne were never parted, and during that time they had a son. But then pirates were seen on the coast, and Finn had to go and fight them. Grainne stayed safe inside her own walls, but just before Finn's return the baby toddled out of the open gate, and Grainne ran after him. As soon as she set foot outside, she turned into a white deer and disappeared with the baby in a swirl of grey mist.

Finn searched for Grainne for ten long years, but he never found even a trace of her until one day his hounds picked up a scent near Grainne's old home. Running behind them, Finn came upon a strange sight. His two fiercest and most loyal hounds were standing in front of a young boy, protecting him from the rest of the pack. "Who are you?" asked Finn. But the boy could only speak the language of a deer, and by that Finn knew that the boy was his lost son.

"I shall call you Oisin, which means Little Deer," he said, hugging him. And Oisin was brought up as a hunter with the Fianna.

Some years after that, the body of a beautiful woman, dressed all in white deerskin was found in the forest, surrounded by a mysterious grey mist. Finn wept many tears over the death of his wife, and he and Oisin and the Fianna dug a grave for her on the top of Hag Mountain. Such was their love for her, that they cast all their jewels in with her, so that she would have a fitting bed to rest on. And so the body of Grainne remains, hidden deep and peaceful, surrounded by a thousand sparkling jewels. And it is said that a mile underneath her grave lies a cave where Finn and Oisin and their men lie in an enchanted sleep until they are woken once more for the defence of Alba.

The wind was rising over the Isle of Eigg, and Coll pulled the boat up the beach. Just then an old man appeared from behind a rock in the cliff. "Come and take shelter," he called. "The storm will be on us soon."

Inside, the old man sat on a ledge, and took out a whistle as thunder drummed above them. "True thunder from Skye," he said, blowing a few notes. "Would you like to be hearing the story of the silver whistle?"

Coll settled himself down near the warmth of the steaming sheep and stroked Branwen's wet feathers. "I would," he said.

◎ 13 ◎

The Silver Whistle

Allan the shepherd whistled like a lark in the spring air. On a night when the Dancing Moon hung low in the sky he was whistling his way back from market, when he came across an old man sitting by a wee fire at the side of the road. "Good evening, Allan," said the old man. "Will you drink a cup of broth with me?" Well, it was a chilly evening, and the fire looked inviting, and soon Allan found himself sitting down with a cup of warm broth in his hands, right in the shadow of Hag Mountain, where Finn and his heroes lie sleeping.

"Now," said the old man. "I hear you are a good whistler, and you must be a brave man to be walking at night with all the ghoulies and ghosties around here. So I'm going to ask you to do a little job for me." He produced a small silver whistle from his pocket, with a cunning pattern that seemed to wriggle in the firelight. Suddenly Allan longed for nothing more than to blow it. "All I want you to do," said the old man, "is to go into that big cave over there, and blow the whistle three times. At the first note a door will open. At the second note you must step forward boldly, and before you sound the third note you must pull your courage round you like a plaid and then blow fearlessly and loud before you can claim your reward."

Allan was so entranced by the little whistle that he agreed without thinking. But as soon as the whistle was in his hands and he was at the mouth of the cave, the fire winked out and the old man disappeared.

"Now that's strange," he said. "But I'll not be boggled by a bit of magic at my age." He drew a deep breath and blew the first note on the silver whistle. Immediately torches blazed, and a great arch appeared, with two huge, carved

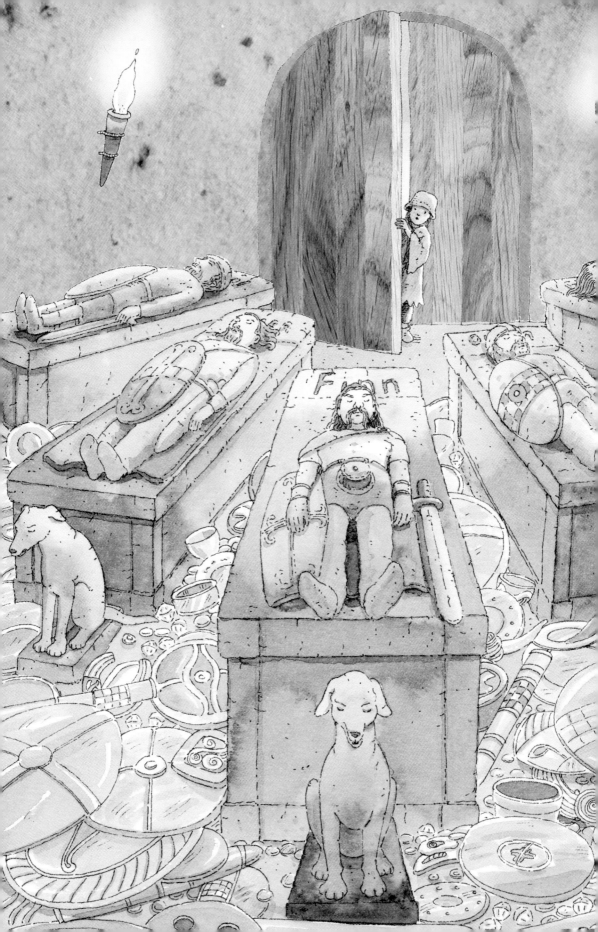

wooden doors in it which began to creak open. Allan tiptoed through them, clutching the whistle in his hand. Inside were many stone beds, each with a gigantic stone warrior lying on it, an enormous hound at his feet. Piles of jewels and gold and silver lay on the floor, sparkling in the light of the torches. There was a name carved above each bed, and Allan went over to have a closer look. Finn, said one. Oisin, said another.

"Maybe I should just let sleeping heroes lie," said Allan, as his heart began to dance a little tippety-tappety rhythm inside his chest. But he drew another deep breath, put the silver whistle to his lips and blew the second note. As he did so, the warriors raised themselves onto their elbows, and the hounds bared their fierce teeth and started to growl.

Fear locked the breath inside Allan's throat, and turned his arms and fingers to jelly, so that he could not have lifted the silver whistle to his lips to sound the third note even if he had wanted to. His feet turned all by themselves and began to run out of the cave, dropping the whistle on the floor as the warriors began to roar and moan. "You're leaving us worse than before! You're leaving us worse than before!"

Allan didn't stay to listen. He ran down the road, away from Hag Mountain, and he never went there again. But the sound of the silver whistle had made Finn and Oisin and their warriors furious. Deafening echoes of their angry shouts rose up out of the top of Hag Mountain and up to the clouds where they got caught in the sky. And whenever there is a storm on Skye, the thunder of their voices is released again. Can you hear them? Listen!

Several days later, Coll and Branwen passed Caliach Point on the north-west corner of Mull. An old woman was hauling lobster creels into a small boat close to the shore.

"She looks older than the Hag of the Ridges," he whispered to Branwen.

"Who's she?" asked the raven.

So, the Hag of the Ridges was Coll's next story.

◎ 14 ◎

The Hag of the Ridges

The Hag of the Ridges came from the north. A whirling cloud of snow froze the deep wrinkles of her blue face, and she stepped on icebergs as she went. On her back she carried a creel of peat, and when she ran out of icebergs, she tipped the peat into the boiling sea and pointed a bony finger at it.

"Be land!" she commanded. And land rose out of the sea – a land full of mountains and lakes and heather. And where the small bits of peat had broken away, islands grew. She smiled a smile full of broken brown teeth. "Mine!" she said, capering from mountain top to mountain top. And wherever her feet trod, the frost took the land in a cold, hard grip.

One morning, as she was dunking her sheets in the fearsome whirlpool of Corryvreckan to get them as white as the snow she loved, she heard singing. As she looked up, a beautiful girl with golden hair walked past her. And wherever the girl's feet trod, small flowers grew in the melting frost. The Hag made a great leap, snatched the girl up into her creel, and then threw her into a cave, where she kept her prisoner.

"You shall not be free until you have washed this brown fleece white," she snarled. "And as I shall give you neither water nor soap, that will be never."

Now the girl was called Grianan, and she was the beloved of Spring. He was very angry when he heard that she was held captive, but although he challenged the Hag of the Ridges again and again, there was no one stronger within the round brown boundaries of earth, and he could never beat her. So he went to see his old friend the Sun.

"Lend me your spear," he begged. "For it is the only thing that will pierce the Hag's cold heart, and make her give my Grianan back to me." But the Sun shook his head.

"Only I can throw my spear," he said. "It is too hot for you to hold. I will make an end of her myself." The Sun harnessed his chariot and drove across the sky. He saw the Hag of the Ridges stumping her way across the moors and straight away he threw his spear at her.

But she heard it coming and dodged under a gorse bush. The spear ploughed a furrow six miles long and six miles wide through the heart of the very earth itself, and made a red-hot blister which burst with a sound like thunder and flung out the Cuillin Hills. The Hag was so weakened by the heat of them that she turned into a pillar of stone for half a year. And it is said that even to this day her snow-covered feet cannot bear to walk on them, even in the depths of winter.

Coll bowed to the full moon shining over Islay as he walked down from the three tall standing stones. Loch Gorm below was green and slimy with weed. Branwen was searching for snails at the water's edge.

"Come away from there or a kelpie will get you," called Coll.

"Tell me a story then," she croaked with her mouth full.

Coll told her a tale of a wife who got the better of a kelpie by simply saying, "Myself is Myself."

◎ 15 ◎

Myself is Myself

There was a wifie who lived by the seashore with her fisherman husband and her three children. She was a hard-working, kind-hearted woman who never let a speck of dirt cross her threshold, nor let a day go by without kissing her children. One day, when her husband was out fishing and her children were out gathering driftwood on the beach, she heard a knock at the door as she was stirring the porridge.

62

"Who's there?" she called, not wanting to leave the porridge in case it burned.

"Only a poor old woman, wanting a wee sup of porridge and a sit by the fire," said a cracked, weaselly voice.

"Well, come you in then, come you in, for I have the porridge on, and the fire burning brightly." At once the door creaked open and an ancient crone hobbled over the threshold. Long grey hair hid her face, and she was dressed in grey-green rags.

Now as the old woman had come in through the door, the wifie had noticed a trail of slimy green footsteps behind her. "A kelpie!" she thought. "A horrible slimy kelpie in my nice clean house!" So when the kelpie asked her name, the wifie knew just what to do.

"Why, I am Myself," she said, and she upended the pot of boiling porridge all over the kelpie's head. The kelpie hopped and screamed and wailed and tore off its nasty old rags as it ran all the way back to its nice cool home under the sea.

"Who has done this dreadful thing to you?" asked the other kelpies, pressing seaweed against its burns, as it danced and gnashed its teeth.

"Myself!" cried the kelpie. "It is Myself!"

"Well," said the other kelpies, shrugging their shoulders, "if you are so stupid as that, then there is nothing more we can do for you." And they left it all alone with its misery. As for the wifie — she had a terrible time getting the green slime and the porridge off her nice clean floor — but she didn't mind a bit.

After a long and stormy sail south, they found themselves at a fort with three large ramparts overlooking Broadsea Bay. Coll had never seen anywhere so big, and was nervous. Branwen dug her beak into his arm. "A bard is welcome anywhere," she scolded.

So Coll climbed up and banged on the wooden door which creaked open slowly. A young warrior peered round suspiciously, but when he saw the harp he smiled. He led Coll and Branwen into a stone hall with a smoky fire blazing in the middle. It was full of warriors and hunting dogs, and sitting closest to the fire on a wooden bench was the laird of the castle with a golden torc round his neck, and blue tattoos on his forearms.

"Welcome," said the laird. "A story might make us all less grumpy now that the winter has put a stop to cattle raiding." So Coll told the tale of the Yellow Giant.

◎ 16 ◎

The Yellow Giant

The maiden Gormshuil of the Fianna had eyes as green as seaweed with the sun on it, hair as dark as peat water at midnight, and skin as pale as the milk from the cow, Grey-Shoulders.

She was so beautiful that she caught the eye of whoever saw her and held their hearts in her hand. However, Gormshuil loved none but the Fianna warrior Caoilte, and none but him would she agree to marry.

One day Gormshuil was playing with the seal pups in their nursery, chasing them in and out of the waves, and laughing her clear, bright laugh at their funny round eyes, and whiskered faces that tickled her legs, when she heard a roar from the islet out in the bay. And from behind a great rock came striding a hideous giant, dressed all in yellow, with a bright yellow face and a bright yellow beard, and bright yellow hairy legs and hands covered in bright yellow warts.

"Disturbing my fishing," he bellowed. "Frightening my food! You'll pay for this!" And he snatched Gormshuil out of the water with a huge yellow hand and strode back to his island, where he imprisoned her in a cave and set her to making birch juice beer and scrubbing the filth of years off the walls and floors.

"You shall be my servant for ever and ever," snarled the giant, whose name was Mochaid.

"Oh no, I shan't!" said Gormshuil, who was brave as well as beautiful. "For Caoilte will come to rescue me, you stupid giant." Now although most giants are stupid, unfortunately Mochaid wasn't one of them. So he lay in wait for Caoilte, who soon came rowing across the bay in his boat to rescue Gormshuil. Instead of challenging him, as

a normal giant would have done, and
receiving an arrow in the eye for his pains,
Mochaid simply gave a slight flick of his
enormous ankle from his hiding place,
and sent a huge boulder soaring across
the water to land plumb smack on poor
Caoilte's head, killing him instantly.
He never even saw it coming.

"Stupid giant, am I?" said Mochaid to Gormshuil as she
wept. "I bet your Caoilte never even told anyone where he
was going." And of course he hadn't. So Mochaid kept
Gormshuil as his servant, to scrub his floors and cook him
enormous stews of fish, and pour him giant tankards of
birch beer until she died of grief — and the Fianna never
found out where either Caoilte or Gormshuil had gone
until many years later, when a wise old raven told them
what had happened and led them to her grave, all covered
in yellow flowers.

"More! More!" shouted the warriors and the laird, stamping their feet. But Coll held up his hand for silence.

"I will gladly tell you all another tale," he said. "But I and my raven are on a secret quest laid on us by the spirits, and so I must ask you a question first. Does one among you know the sea ways to Manannan's Isle? And if so, would that one be willing to guide me there? I need to find a wizard called Broc, who has travelled in the south."

There was a cough at the back of the hall, and the young gate guard stood up.

"I am Finbar," he said. "I come from Ellan Vannin, which is Manannan's Isle, and Broc is my father. I will guide you there if my laird will give me leave."

The laird grunted. "Who am I to defy the will of the spirits?" he asked. "But mind you're back soon, Finbar. I'll need your spear when the cattle raiding starts. Now, what about that tale?"

"Listen then," said Coll, "and I will tell you the story of Geal, Donn and Critheanach."

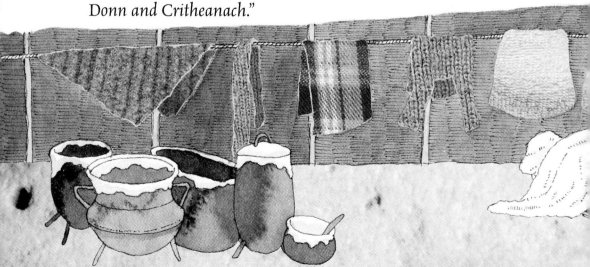

17

Bright Geal, Brown Donn and Lovely Critheanach

There was an old laird who had three beautiful daughters, all born on one Midsummer's night at the cost of their mother's life. The eldest, Geal, was bright as stars, the next, Donn, was brown as a shining river in spate, and Critheanach the youngest was so lovely that she made men tremble at the sight of her. The old laird was very sad indeed at his wife's death and he retired into his strong-room to count his precious gold, leaving the three girls to be brought up by servants.

The two elder girls grew up shrill and bold, and they bullied their younger sister unmercifully, making her do all the hard work in the house. Poor Critheanach found herself scrubbing pots, and sweeping floors and mending clothes while Geal and Donn swept about the house giving orders and shouting. Soon her loveliness was quite disguised by dirt and smuts and rags.

Now every Saturday there was a great fair at Stranraer, where all the young women of a certain age went to show off their fine clothes and, perhaps, to find a husband. As soon as they were allowed, Geal and Donn went every Saturday, but it never occurred to them that Critheanach might want to come too.

"Mend my blue dress by the time I'm back," said Donn.

"Mind the kitchen is clean by my return," said Geal. And off they rode with a clatter of hooves on the roadway while poor Critheanach watched them go.

Just then an old woman dressed in a brown cloak popped out from behind a bush.

"Would you like to buy a charm, my dear?" she asked.

"I should love to," she said. "But my sisters have taken all the money in the house to go to the fair."

"And why aren't you there too, young Critheanach? You are the right age, aren't you?" asked the old woman (whose name was Baobh, and who, as you might have guessed, was a fairy).

Critheanach laughed wistfully. "How I wish I could go," she sighed. "But I have mending and cleaning to do, and besides, I have no clothes to wear."

Baobh sniffed disapprovingly. "We'll see about that," she said, and she waved her crooked heather walking stick in a cunning little circle in the air.

Ziiipp! Critheanach was dressed from head to toe in heather purple, with shoes as green as myrtle leaves. A white mare with silver harness bells stood in the roadway waiting for her.

"Off you go to the fair, my dear," said Baobh. "I shall take care of the cleaning and mending. But mind you don't speak to your sisters, or to any young gentlemen, and come back after an hour as quick as the horse can gallop." So Critheanach went to the fair and marvelled at all the sights. She did exactly as Baobh had said, and although she saw Geal and Donn, she didn't speak to them, nor to any of the many young men who tried to catch her attention. As soon as the hour had struck she galloped home. Just as she arrived at the door and dismounted, her fine clothes turned to rags again, but as Baobh had promised, all the work had been done.

Soon Geal and Donn were home too, talking of nothing but the beautiful lady who had been at the fair, and demanding their father sell some of his precious gold to buy them dresses as fine as hers.

The next Saturday Geal and Donn rode out in their new dresses calling instructions and commands behind them, but Critheanach stayed at home as usual.

"What! Haven't you gone too?" asked Baobh, popping out from behind the bush again.

Critheanach smiled sadly. "I have no dress, and there is still housework to be done," she said.

"Tish and tush," snorted Baobh. And she waved her heather stick again. This time Critheanach was dressed in a dress as red as holly berries, with a cloak like newly churned cream. The white mare with the silver bells carried Critheanach to the fair as before, Baobh's words ringing in her ears. "Mind you don't speak to your sisters, or to any young gentlemen, and come back after an hour as quick as the horse can gallop."

But Baobh hadn't reckoned with Duncan, the young prince of Kilbrannan, who saw Critheanach and fell madly in love with her at that very same minute.

Although she would not speak to him,
he ran beside her as she turned for home, and as she
urged the white mare to a gallop, he seized one of her shoes.

"I shall not rest until I find the woman who fits this
shoe," he cried, "even if I have to try it on every woman in the
land around. And when I have found her I shall marry her."

Geal and Donn came home buzzing with news of the
young prince's words. "We must have new dresses for Prince
Duncan's visit," they said. "For this shoe must fit one of us."
Sure enough, after a few days, the prince came knocking at
the door. The two sisters immediately locked Critheanach
in the kitchen, and went to greet him. But when the shoe
(being a fairy shoe which would fit none but its true owner)
did not fit either Geal or Donn, they fell into a rage of
screaming and wailing, so that the old laird came out of his
strongroom to see what was the matter.

"But where is my third daughter?" he asked, when
things had been explained to him. "Why has she not tried
on the shoe?"

"I did not know you had a third daughter," said Prince Duncan. "Let her be brought." So Critheanach was let out from the kitchen, and as soon as she tried on the shoe, it naturally fitted her, all her rags and grime fell away, and Prince Duncan recognised her as his lost love. Luckily Critheanach had fallen in love with him at once too, so nine days later they were married. Everyone was happy but Geal and Donn.

"I should have been married first, I'm the eldest," sulked Geal.

"Who will do our mending now?" brooded Donn. And they began to plot and scheme to kill their sister. Some days after the wedding, they came upon Critheanach walking along the cliff top, and they rushed at her and threw her over. Luckily Critheanach's cloak caught on the wind and carried her gently down to the waves, just where a big whale was yawning. She landed on his soft tongue and was swallowed in a minute.

"That's the end of her," said Geal and Donn, and they decided that Geal should take Critheanach's place. However, Prince Duncan was not deceived, and soon his sword was at Geal's throat as he demanded to know where his bride was.

"In a whale's belly," said Geal, "and you will never get her back from there." But Prince Duncan was a determined man, and he rowed out into the ocean and asked every sea creature if they had seen or heard of his Critheanach. Soon enough he met the King of the Whales, who opened his mouth, and there, sitting on his tongue, was Critheanach. Oh, how happy they were to see each other!

And as for Geal and Donn, they were sent out to sea in a boat with no oars, and left to the mercy of Manannan the sea god. Some say a kelpie found them and took them undersea to be his slaves. I do not know if that is the truth of it, but I do hope so.

The Ellan Vannin Stories

The streaming sleet ran down the sail and down their frozen necks. They were very close to Ellan Vannin but the wind had turned against them, and they didn't dare sail closer to the sharp rocks that ringed the island, now hidden in a heavy mist.

"Manannan's fog," said Finbar. "It often hides the island for days at a time at this season. Maybe if you gave the god a story, he would let us through."

So Coll told the story of the ben-varrey, the beautiful sea maid.

❧ 18 ❧

The Ben-Varrey

Odo Paden cast out his nets for the last time. They would be empty again, he just knew it. And they were. He sighed as he stowed the nets away. It would be a hungry night. Just then he heard a thump on the keel, and looking up he saw a young ben-varrey sitting on the edge of the boat. She was very beautiful, as sea maids usually are, and she was smiling at him.

"Cast your nets out again, Odo Paden, and if they are full you shall marry me."

Odo Paden looked at her grumpily. "What use is a ben-varrey as a wife?" he asked. "You can't even walk on land."

"Just do it," said the ben-varrey. "And you will see." So Odo Paden cast out his nets once more, and when he pulled them in, they were full of fish, including a large silver sea-trout.

"You must take the silver trout and sell it at market for a gold sovereign," said the ben-varrey. "Then you must stand at the top of the Rock of Drowning and throw it into the sea. Only then will I be able to walk on land and marry you." So Odo Paden put the trout in his sack and went to market.

But when he got there, there was a big crowd around a showman, and in front of the showman was a cat with a fiddle. As the cat played, a mouse and a cockroach danced with each other.

"What a marvel," said Odo Paden.

"Indeed it is," said the showman. "But I will only sell them to the man who can give me a silver sea-trout. I just fancy a nice baked sea-trout for my supper." Odo Paden pulled out his fish.

"I was going to sell it for a gold sovereign," he said.

"You will have many gold sovereigns if you buy my little friends," said the showman. "It's a once in a lifetime opportunity." So Odo Paden handed over the fish and took the cat and fiddle, the cockroach and the mouse home with him in his sack.

"Oh, Odo Paden," said the ben-varrey sadly, when he showed her what he had bought. "Now you have ruined my only chance of escaping the wicked wizard Drogh-Yantagh. I am a princess, but I would still have married you and made you happy if you had rescued me by throwing the gold sovereign off the Rock of Drowning. Now my only chance is that someone will make the wizard laugh three times. And that will be never, for Drogh-Yantagh is cruel and has no sense of humour at all." Then she disappeared back into the sea.

Odo Paden felt terrible. He leapt up and stuffing his purchases back into his sack, he set off towards the Rock of Drowning and marched right up to the top of it.

"Drogh-Yantagh!" he shouted. "I have come to make you laugh!" All at once a dreadful black figure was towering over him.

"I may laugh already, little mortal, when I see you standing there so brave and alone! What do you want from me?" said a deep, dark voice.

"I want you to let the ben-varrey princess go!" said Odo Paden fiercely. And all at once, the ben-varrey was sitting on the rock beside the wizard.

"What have you done?" she said. "Your life is in terrible danger." But Odo Paden didn't care. He pulled out the cat and fiddle, and when it started to play, Drogh-Yantagh let out a bark of laughter.

"One!" said Odo Paden. Then he let out the mouse and the cockroach. As soon as they started to dance, the wizard laughed again.

"Two!" said Odo Paden. Then the mouse tripped over the cockroach and fell down. The wizard laughed as if he would never stop.

"And that's three!" said Odo Paden. As he spoke, the ben-varrey grew two beautiful long legs, and stepped onto the rock beside him. Drogh-Yantagh let out a cry of rage.

"To think that I should be tricked by a cat, a mouse and a cockroach," he screamed over the wind. But as he spoke a fiery chasm opened at his feet and swallowed him up. For as every sailor on Ellan Vannin knows, those three words may never be uttered by a wizard at sea. As for Odo Paden and his princess, they went to live in her father's castle after they were married. Odo Paden became king of the island in time, and a very good one he made too.

At last, the mist cleared, the sleet stopped, and a soft sunlight fell on Ellan Vannin, lighting up the green hills till they glowed like jewels.

"There is Laxey harbour," cried Finbar. "And I can see my father waiting on the shore."

The boat drew up on the sand, and Broc, a tall man in brown robes, came to meet them. "My warrior son," he said, as Finbar hugged him. "And a new friend. A young man in search of knowledge if I am not mistaken. I know why you are here, young Coll. My magic pool of seeing shows me many things. I saw your meeting with my old friend Donall Mhor, but I saw you even before that, on a dark night of fire when the spirits called a young man to his quest. But I have not been where you are going, nor do I know where it is. In the morning we will ask my pool of seeing what it can tell us. Come on in and get warm. Then you can give us a story."

So when he had dried his harp out, Coll told the story of the Hag's long bag and the stolen gold.

❧ 19 ❧

The Hag's Long Bag

A poor widow from Ellan Vannin had three daughters, Callybrid, Callyphony, and Callyvorra. Her husband had left her all right and tight, with a little cottage, and a little bag of gold which she kept in a long leather bag, hidden under the hearthstone for emergencies. One day there was a knock on the door, and there stood an old woman.

"Will you give me a bit of soup?" mumbled the old woman. So the widow poured a bowl of soup and went to get a bit of bread from the crock to go with it. When she turned round, quick as a flash the old woman had disappeared, the hearthstone lay open wide, and the gold had gone.

"I shall go out to work," said Callybrid. "And I shall send my wages back." So her mother baked a special oatcake.

"You may have the whole oatcake and no blessing, or a blessing and a bit taken out," said the widow. And Callybrid decided on the whole oatcake. Off she went, and a long while later she came to a cave where an old hag woman was coughing and sweeping, coughing and sweeping the dust.

"You look as if you could do with some help," said Callybrid. The old woman agreed that she could, so Callybrid was hired as a maid.

"But just one thing," said the old hag woman. "You must never take even the smallest peep up my chimney." And Callybrid agreed that she wouldn't. However, by the evening she couldn't resist, and when the old woman had gone out to gather herbs, she took a tiny peep. Right there, hanging in the chimney, was her mother's very own long leather bag of gold, but much fuller than before. Callybrid grabbed it and rushed out of the cave towards home.

"Groom me, groom me," neighed a chestnut horse on the way. But Callybrid was in too much of a hurry.

"Tie me, tie me," bleated a wandering goat on the way. But Callybrid was in too much of a hurry.

"Milk me, milk me," mooed a brindle cow on the way. But Callybrid was in too much of a hurry.

"Shear me, shear me," baaed a black sheep on the way. But Callybrid was in too much of a hurry.

"Turn me, turn me," groaned a millstone as Callybrid ran into the millhouse. But she was too exhausted, and she fell asleep on a sack of flour. Meanwhile the old hag woman had discovered her loss, and with a scream of rage she came whirling and twirling, twirling and whirling down the road on her bristlebrush broom.

"Have you seen a girl with a long leather bag?" she snarled at all the animals.

"Yes," they all replied. "She went that way." Soon enough she discovered Callybrid asleep and turned her into a millstone.

Some months later when the widow and her two daughters were becoming very thin and hungry, and there was no news from Callybrid, Callyphony decided to go out to work. She too took the special oatcake and no blessing, and she trod the same path to the old hag woman's door as her sister, and she too ended up as a millstone.

Winter was coming on, with no news of either Callybrid or Callyphony, and the widow and Callyvorra had no money to buy warm clothes. "I shall go out to work now," said Callyvorra. "But I shall take less oatcake and your blessing." So she set out in the cold wind, and and a long while later she came to a cave where an old hag woman was coughing and sweeping, coughing and sweeping the dust.

"You look as if you could do with some help," said Callyvorra. The old woman agreed that she could, so Callyvorra was hired as a maid.

"But just one thing," said the old hag woman. "You must never take even the smallest peep up my chimney." And Callybrid agreed that she wouldn't. However, by the evening she couldn't resist, and when the old woman had gone out to gather herbs, she took a tiny peep. Right there, hanging in the chimney, was her mother's very own long leather bag of gold, but much fuller than before. Callyvorra grabbed it and rushed out of the cave towards home.

"Groom me, groom me," neighed a chestnut horse on the way. So Callyvorra groomed him.

"Tie me, tie me," bleated a wandering goat on the way. So Callyvorra tied her.

"Milk me, milk me," mooed a brindle cow on the way. So Callyvorra milked her.

"Shear me, shear me," baaed a black ram on the way. So Callyvorra sheared him.

"Turn me, turn me," groaned a millstone as Callybrid ran into the millhouse. So she set the millstones turning before she fell asleep on a sack of flour. Meanwhile the old hag woman had discovered her loss, and with a scream of rage she came whirling and twirling, twirling and whirling down the road on her bristlebrush broom.

"Have you seen a girl with a long leather bag?" she snarled at all the animals.

"No, we haven't," they said.

But eventually the old hag woman arrived at the millhouse. "Have you seen a girl with a long leather bag," she snarled.

"Come closer," groaned the millstone, "and I will tell you." As she leaned forward,

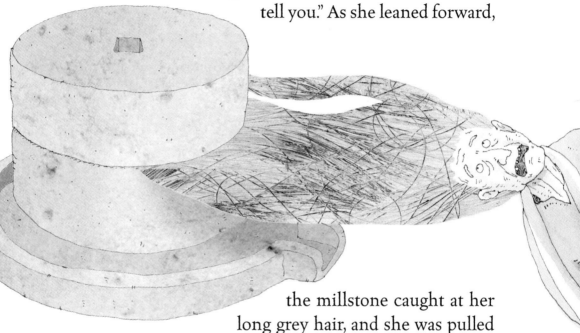

the millstone caught at her long grey hair, and she was pulled into the wheel and ground up tinier than dust.

When Callyvorra woke up, the millstone told her what had happened, and told her to touch the two stones in the corner with the old hag woman's bristlebrush broom. What rejoicing there was when the three sisters went home to their mother, carrying the long leather bag between them. And it is said that if you listen to a certain mill on Ellan Vannin to this very day, in the grinding of the stones you can hear the old hag groaning and gnashing her teeth at the loss of all that gold.

The last echo of Coll's voice died away into the embers of the fire, and Broc sighed contentedly. "It's good to know that Ollach still teaches the stories of Ellan Vannin to his pupils," he said. "He even taught me, once. And now it is my turn to tell you a story of this island. Fingal, bring my harp." Fingal stood up and brought his father a small wooden harp, carved with cats, and Broc struck a chord and began the story of brave Marown and the hideous Buggane.

❋ 20 ❋

Marown and the Buggane

There was a man called Marown who sewed clothes for a living. Deerskin or linen, tunics or fine robes, it made no difference to his flying fingers. He was a boastful fellow, who liked to drink heather ale, and tell tall tales to his friends.

"Why," he lied one dark night, as he was drinking with the young warriors of the tribe, "I even spent a night with the Buggane of Keeil Brisht once. It didn't frighten me at all, oh no."

"I bet you wouldn't do it again, though," said one of the men.

"Wouldn't I just," said Marown. "How much do you bet?" So the men whispered among themselves, as men do, with much nudging and winking, and then they said that they would bet him four gold pieces and a boar's tusk drinking horn if he would do it.

"Done," hiccupped Marown, who had by now had more ale than was good for him, "and I'll have a kiss from the chieftain's daughter as well."

"Right," said the young warriors, winking and nudging some more. "We'll be going there now, shall we?" Marown gulped, suddenly sober. He realised that his boastful talk had got him into real trouble this time. But there was no escaping. He would have to go and spend a night with the dreadful Buggane of Keeil Brisht. He would probably be terrified to death and then eaten. That was what usually happened.

The young warriors bundled him up to Keeil Brisht and shoved him inside. Then they ran to the bottom of the hill to wait for the dawn. Poor Marown shivered and shook. But as night wore on and nothing happened he calmed down a bit.

"If I get my needle and thread out, and sew a fancy pattern onto my cloak, I can look at that and nothing else, and if the Buggane comes, perhaps I shan't be so frightened," he said to himself. So he took out his needle and thread, lit a candle stub and started to sew with trembling fingers. Just then a moaning and a groaning and a grumbling came from under the earth and a hollow voice cried out:

"Who has come to disturb my rest? Do you know who I am, foolish mortal?"

"Yes," said Marown, sewing faster. "You are the Buggane of Keeil Brisht."

"And I suppose you think you aren't going to be terrified of me?" said the Buggane, sliding a black hairy hand with long red talons out of the earth. Marown sewed even faster.

"Oh, I'm sure I shall be," he said in a bored voice. The Buggane was taken aback.

"Do you know that the sight of me turns people blind and scares them to death," boomed the Buggane,

sliding his horned head with its fiery saucer eyes out of the ground. Marown sewed till his fingers were a flash of lightning over the material of his cloak. He glanced at the east, which was becoming lighter.

"I'm sure it does," he said. "In fact I'm practically afraid myself." The Buggane was getting really annoyed now. It began to grind its teeth.

"Do you hear that?" it asked. "That's my teeth that are sharper than razors. My teeth that can cut you in two WITH JUST ONE BITE!" Marown was sewing so fast now that you couldn't even see his fingers. He glanced to the east again and saw the welcome red flush of the sun on the horizon.

"I'll just bet they can," he said, getting to his feet and running for the door with his cloak flapping behind him. "But I'm not staying to find out." And do you know, the Buggane couldn't follow him, because the sun had now risen and it had to return to the depths of the earth, as angry as a swarm of wasps in a jar.

Marown won his bet, and claimed his gold, his drinking horn and his kiss. But he never went near Keeil Brisht again.

The next day, as they stared at Broc's magic pool, a silver mist started to rise. Coll looked in and saw a tall green hill. "My vision of Wintereve!" he exclaimed.

"Hush," said Broc. "Let us see if there is more." Suddenly a series of pictures chased each other across the surface of the pool – three old women spinning, a man with fire spouting from his head, a golden-haired woman veiled in black, a golden holly berry – so many that Coll could barely keep up. Then the pool went dark and rain stippled its surface.

"I shall have to think on this," said Broc. "Finbar, look after Coll and bring him back to me on Longnight." And he left the grove.

"Come on," said Finbar. "I know a perfect place to get away from the rain. And I'll tell you about Chalse and the Foawr while we're going there. It's the only story I know."

❧ 21 ❧

Chalse and the Foawr

There was a young man called Chalse who was a fiddler by trade, and not a very good one. *Scrape, scrape, squeak, squeak* went his bow across the strings until the noise drove his family and his neighbours and his friends nearly mad. "You're only fit to play to the Foawr," they said. "And even they would throw you out."

"They would not," said Chalse. "And since you don't seem to appreciate my music, to the Foawr I shall go." And he did, tramping over all the island till he came to where the Foawr spent their time rolling great rocks and boulders into the sea for fun. Chalse sat on a rock and started to play. *Scrape, scrape, squeak, squeak* went his bow across the strings, until almost all the Foawr put their enormous hands over their enormous ears and ran back to their caves. There was just one Foawr who did not run away. And he lumbered across to Chalse and picked him up in one enormous hand.

"I like your scraping and squeaking, little fiddler," he said. "But then I'm a teensy bit deaf. I shall take you home to my cave and you shall play for me some more before I eat you for my supper." Now this was not at all what Chalse had intended and he was very frightened. But he kept his wits about him.

"If you ate one of those fat sheep over there for supper," he shouted, pointing to the nearby hillside. "I could play for you for two nights instead of one." The Foawr thought about this for a while.

"That's a good idea," he said. "I wish I had more good ideas, but I'm too stupid. The other Foawr all laugh at me." And he began to cry fat, wet tears that fell onto his hand and soaked Chalse to the skin.

When the Foawr had eaten his sheep supper (and a messy business it was), he rolled the stone across the cave mouth. "That's to stop you escaping, little human," he said. "I'm not that stupid! You can play me to sleep now." So Chalse scraped and squeaked away, and eventually the Foawr began to snore. Chalse began to explore the cave, and soon he found a narrow chimney leading out to the clifftop above. Up and up he climbed, and he ran all the way home as fast as he could.

"Did the Foawr throw you out then?" asked his family, sleepily, as he crept through the door.

"No," said Chalse, shivering at the memory. "But I wish they had. I wish they had."

They spent the nights in the warm wool shed which smelt of wet sheep. Coll and Finbar lay on piles of fleeces as they waited for evening. "All this wool reminds me of another story," said Coll. "Do you want to hear the tale of Old Woman Big Foot?"

"Of course I do," said Finbar. "It's not often I get my own personal bard, you know!"

❧ 22 ❧

Old Woman Big Foot

Pignut was the laziest girl in the world, and also the most beautiful. If there were dishes to do, she did them so slowly that she drove her mother nearly mad. If there was washing to do it took her all afternoon. If there were sheep to herd, she let them wander where they liked while she slept under a tree. And if she was left to watch a pot on the stove, she burned it.

"What shall I do with you, you great lazy lump of beauty?" shouted her mother in despair, at least twenty times a day. One day, just as the shearing was finished, Pignut's mother was scolding her once again when the king came riding by.

"Why must you scold this beautiful girl so?" he said.

"Oh, your majesty," said the mother, thinking fast. "I was just telling her she works too hard. Why, she was about to comb all these fleeces smooth and spin them into fine woollen thread in a single day."

"Now that is amazing," said the king. "You must let your daughter come home with me to the palace. I think she would make me a good queen if she can really do that." Well! What could the mother do except let poor Pignut get up behind the king and ride to his palace?

The king gave Pignut a good supper and sent her to bed early, and the next day he locked her in a little room with several fleeces, some combs and a spinning wheel. "I shall come back tonight and see how you've got on," he said. Now Pignut was not very good at combing the wool smooth, let alone spinning it into fine woollen thread, so she started to cry. But as the tears fell on her knees, she felt

a pat on the shoulder. An old woman with
enormous rough hands and gigantic
feet was standing there.

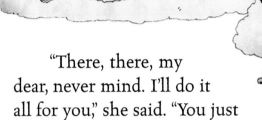

"There, there, my
dear, never mind. I'll do it
all for you," she said. "You just
go and have a nap on that wool
over there." Pignut was too astonished to speak, so she did as
she was told, and when she woke up as the sun was setting,
there were hundreds of little bundles of fine woollen
thread, all stacked neatly on the floor.

"How can I ever repay you?" she gasped. The old
woman smiled, her long red nose wrinkling.

"You can invite me to your wedding," she said. "Just
give the invitation to the nearest seagull, addressed to Aunt
Bigfoot." So Pignut agreed gladly.

The king was so pleased with her work that the
wedding invitations were sent out the very next day, and
Pignut made quite sure that she kept her promise. After the
wedding, when everyone had arrived, and the king and his
new queen were greeting their guests, there in front of
them stood the old woman. "And who is this, my dear?"
asked the king.

"I am the queen's Aunt Bigfoot," said the old woman. "It's me she gets her spinning skills. See my big feet?" She lifted her skirt so the king could see them and they were TRULY enormous. "That's from treadling the spinning wheel. See my rough old hands?" And she held them out to the king and they were VERY rough. "That's from combing the wool. See my red nose?" The king nodded – it was HORRIBLY red. "That's from bending over the thread. Pignut will get just like me if she carries on spinning."

Needless to say, the king rather liked Pignut as she was, so he forbade her ever to spin again, and she lived the rest of her life in lazy luxury, just as she preferred.

As Coll, Branwen and Finbar returned to the now dark pool on Longnight, Broc sighed. "It has been a long, hard day of scrying a path for you. I have seen many strange signs and portents and I am still lacking some answers. But the Otherworld spirits tell me that you must seek Brehanna of the Golden Herds in the land of the Children of Danu. The high, green hill of Tara is her home, although it is not the hill you have seen in your vision. Nevertheless, it is she who holds one of the keys to your quest. Tonight is Longnight, and you must be with her by Imbolc, the Feast of New Ewes' Milk. One more thing. You will face a magical test before you can reach her. Beware the red mists." Then Coll and Finbar helped Broc home for the Longnight celebration feast. There was a lot of ale and Coll told many stories. But the best one of all was the story of Gilaspick Qualtrough, who had a bet with the god Manannan.

❧ 23 ❧

Gilaspick Qualtrough

Gilaspick Qualtrough the fisherman told the tallest stories in all Manannan's Isle. He had sailed the furthest, he had caught the biggest fish, he had seen the scariest sea monsters. But the trouble was, no one believed him.

None of this dented Gilaspick Qualtrough's fine opinion of himself. "Ho ho!" he said as he walked towards the ale house. "What a clever fellow I am."

The alehouse was full, and there was just one seat left, next to a stranger. "Hello, my friend," said Gilaspick. "I am Gilaspick Qualtrough, and if you buy me a drink, I'll tell you all about my extraordinary adventures. Why, I've sailed to places you've never even dreamed of." The stranger looked at him.

"I'll bet you've never sailed to Fingal," he said. Gilaspick had never heard of Fingal, but he certainly wasn't going to admit *that*.

"Fingal!" he said. "Why getting there is not near so dangerous as the sail from Maughold Head down to Cronk Karren. I bet I could do it, easy!" The stranger smiled wickedly.

"Very well, Gilaspick Qualtrough. I bet you that you cannot sail to Fingal and back before the moon is next full, and bring me the Belle of Ballakissack to prove that you've been there. If you fail, you will forfeit everything you own." Now Gilaspick wasn't a man to refuse a bet, so he held out his hand to the stranger.

"Done!" he said boastfully. But next morning his heart was in his boots. He had no idea how far Fingal was, or how he would know when he had got there, let alone if he could get there and back by the next full moon.

"Don't forget to bring me the Belle of Ballakissack," called the stranger as Gilaspick sailed out of the harbour and let the wind take him where it would.

Gilaspick had been sailing for what seemed like days, when he ran into a dense silvery mist. When it cleared, he saw a sandy beach in front of him and an old woman in a blue cloak picking seaweed. "Good day," he said politely. "Where am I?"

The old woman shook her finger at him. "Why, this is Fingal, of course," she said. "And where have you come from not to be knowing that?"

"I have come from Manannan's Isle to bring back the Belle of Ballakissack for a bet," said Gilaspick Qualtrough. Then he thought for a minute. "Er . . . would you be knowing what exactly *is* it, and where I would be finding it?" The old woman cackled scornfully.

"The Belle is a she, not an it, young man. And you will be finding her up that path, in the king's palace. But I don't think you will find it an easy matter to steal her."

So Gilaspick went up the path, and soon he found himself in a palace, surrounded by people all dressed in silks and satins. There was a party going on, and everyone was dancing happily except for one beautiful girl who was sobbing in a corner. He stopped by an old woman in a red shawl. "What's going on?" he asked. "And why is that girl so unhappy?"

"Ah, my son," she said. "That is the king's daughter, the Belle of Ballakissack, and she is unhappy because today she is to marry the wicked sorcerer Prince Imshee so that the curse can be taken off her father's kingdom." Then she disappeared into the crowd. Gilaspick went over to the princess.

"Excuse me, lady, but are you the Belle of Ballakissack?" he asked. The princess raised blue eyes as full of tears as a lake in spring.

"Yes," she sniffed.

"Then I've come to take you away," said Gilaspick. And with that he whirled her into the dance, out of the door, and down the sandy path to his boat. Just as they set sail, there was a tremendous shouting, and looking back they saw a wizened little man with a bulbous nose and a warty face leap onto a hazel branch as if it were a horse and soar up into the sky.

"Oh no!" said the Belle. "That is Prince Imshee. Now we will never escape." But Gilaspick had not lived on Manannan's Isle all his life without knowing what he must do.

"Manannan Mac Lir!" he cried. "God of the sea! Cover us with your cloak, I beg you." And immediately a heavy sea fog covered them. Gilaspick felt the wind at his back, and before he could think how strange it was that the fog did not disappear with the wind, the sail had filled and they were racing over the waves. In no time at all they had come to a desolate island with a beach of black sand, where an old woman in a blue cloak was sitting on a rock.

"I have no idea where we are," admitted Gilaspick.

"More fool you," said the old woman disagreeably. "This is Imshee's Isle, and he won't be pleased that you have stolen his bride." There was a roar of rage and the hideous sorcerer landed behind them. The Belle started to sob.

"Shut up, you," said the sorcerer, pointing his wand at her throat and taking her voice, "and as for you, fisherman, did you really think your ocean god could save you from ME?" He aimed a bolt of lightning at Gilaspick and threw him backwards.

"Save me, Manannan," cried Gilaspick. But nothing happened. Prince Imshee advanced on the Belle with his hands outstretched. Gilaspick couldn't bear it. "I thought you were supposed to come in person to protect your sons, Manannan, you old fraud!" he cried.

"And so I do," remarked a great voice out of the waves. "Even when they fail to remember that they have to call on me three times before I can help them on the land. Now take the girl and go while I deal with this nasty little sorcerer." Gilaspick fled to his boat, dragging the silent Belle behind him, and set sail just as Manannan sank Prince Imshee and his black island into the depths of the sea.

They landed on a little green island at sunset to rest for the night. "How are we going to get your voice back?" said Gilaspick. Just then an old woman in a violet cloak came towards them.

"I am Aileen the healer, and I have something that will help," she said. And she was quite right. By the morning the Belle had her voice back.

"How can we thank you?" asked Gilaspick.

"Just remember, if you see an old herb woman, be kind and buy something from her," said the old woman. "Now be on your way. The moon will be full tomorrow." Gilaspick suddenly remembered the stranger and his bet. By now he had fallen in love with the Belle of Ballakissack and he didn't want to let her go. As they sailed towards Manannan's Isle together, he discovered that she loved him right back, even if he was a poor fisherman.

"But you must keep your side of the bargain," she said. "Otherwise you will lose everything." As they walked up towards the alehouse, they passed an old herbwoman setting out her stall.

"Buy a little something," she quavered. And Gilaspick remember the healer's words and bought a little green bag.

"Though I do not think it will help a broken heart," he said to the Belle. The old woman just winked. As they reached the alehouse, they saw the stranger sitting on the bench outside.

"Well? Have you been to Fingal and brought me the Belle of Ballakissack?" he asked. Gilaspick pulled the Belle closer to his side.

"Yes," he said. "I have. But we love each other and I do not want to let her go. I will fight you for her." The stranger laughed.

"I don't think so," he said. "But I will take a bag of dried sea poppies for her." Now dried sea poppies are the rarest thing there is, and Gilaspick knew he had no chance at all. But the Belle stepped forward.

"We only have this, sir," she said, putting the herbwoman's little green bag into his hand. And as the stranger opened it, Gilaspick saw that it *was* dried sea poppies. His mouth fell open.

"A bargain is a bargain," said the stranger. "I am so glad I chose you for this task, Gilaspick Qualtrough." Gilaspick's mouth fell open still further, for the stranger was growing bigger, and a silver chariot of oystershells drawn by white foaming sea horses was coming up from the sea. The stranger stepped into it and whirled away into the ocean. "Goodbye, my son and my new daughter," said Manannan Mac Lir.

Gilaspick didn't mind too much when nobody believed his latest tall story. He was too busy being happy with his new bride.

Stories from Eriu

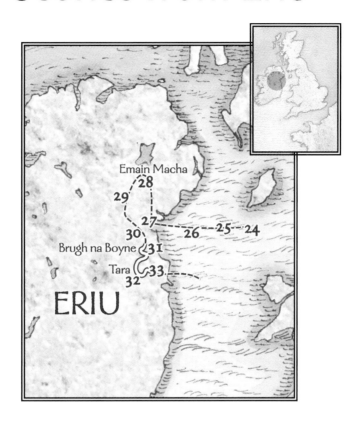

It was time to set sail again to Eriu from Laxey Harbour. Coll rubbed his aching head as Branwen cackled. "You always drink too much ale on Longnight. Ravens are more sensible!" He stowed his harp in the boat and turned to say goodbye to Broc and Finbar.

"Remember that Eriu is a strange place," said Broc. "It is under the protection of the children of Danu still, even though they have retired to the Otherworld. Remind yourself of them as you sail, for they have many tricks."

"I will," said Coll. "I shall tell Branwen the story as we go. It will pass the time."

⊹ 24 ⊹

The Children of Danu

In the cauldron of the universe the black soup of being brewed and bubbled. And in the first moment when time existed, the cauldron boiled over, spilling onto the dark body of earth, filling her seas and lakes and rivers with the sacred waters of Danu the Mother Goddess.

Soon a great tree God grew up from the earth, and his name was Bilé. He was tall and strong, and his leaves

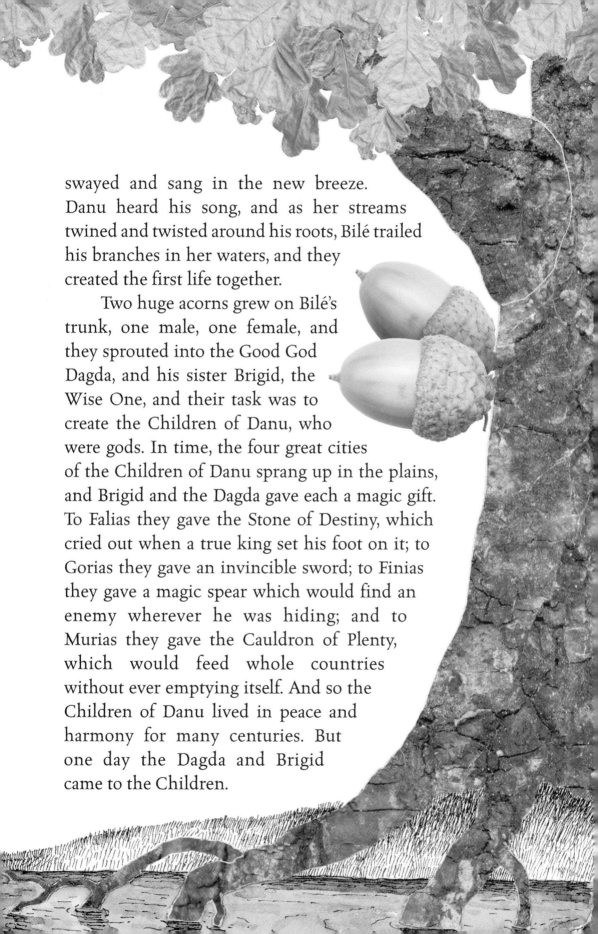

swayed and sang in the new breeze.
Danu heard his song, and as her streams
twined and twisted around his roots, Bilé trailed
his branches in her waters, and they
created the first life together.

Two huge acorns grew on Bilé's
trunk, one male, one female, and
they sprouted into the Good God
Dagda, and his sister Brigid, the
Wise One, and their task was to
create the Children of Danu, who
were gods. In time, the four great cities
of the Children of Danu sprang up in the plains,
and Brigid and the Dagda gave each a magic gift.
To Falias they gave the Stone of Destiny, which
cried out when a true king set his foot on it; to
Gorias they gave an invincible sword; to Finias
they gave a magic spear which would find an
enemy wherever he was hiding; and to
Murias they gave the Cauldron of Plenty,
which would feed whole countries
without ever emptying itself. And so the
Children of Danu lived in peace and
harmony for many centuries. But
one day the Dagda and Brigid
came to the Children.

"Bilé and Danu have told us that you must follow the path of the setting sun to the land of Eriu, which you must fill with people. The earth there is lonely, and longs to hear the laughter of human children. But beware: you may have to fight when you get there, because it is the place of Danu's dark sister, Domnu, and she and her family will not be pleased to see you." So the Children of Danu packed up their treasures and their cities, and whirled away westward across the ocean in a silver cloud of raindrops.

When they landed on the southern shores of Eriu they saw that it was a green land, of rounded hills and soft mists. Sure enough, there lived the Firbolgs, the children of Domnu, and they were not at all happy with their visitors.

"Let us drive them out," shouted their king, Eochaid the Arrogant, and so there was a great battle. Nuada, king of the Children of Danu, lost his hand in the savage fighting, but eventually the Firbolgs were defeated. Nuada Silver-Hand gave them the land of Connaught to be their own, because they had fought so bravely.

In the north of Eriu lived the giants from the sea. The Children of Danu were tired of fighting, so they made an alliance with the giants and their leader, Balor One-Eye. But the giants were greedy and mean, and soon Nuada and his people were at war again. They had on their side the great

sun god Lugh Long-Arm, but he was a man of so many talents that Nuada decided not to risk him in battle, and put him under guard so he couldn't join in. After many days of fighting, the giants overcame all the magic gifts which the Dagda had given their enemies, and threw their troops across the plain of Moytura against the Children of Danu in a thunder of tramping feet. Many brave ones fell that morning, and Balor One-Eye killed Nuada himself. All was going very badly for the Children of Danu. But suddenly a streak of light came winging across the plain. It was Lugh. Everyone stopped fighting.

"Balor One-Eye," he cried. "I challenge you!"

Balor turned to his companions. "Let me look at this boaster!" he grunted. So the giants around him took an iron hook and started to haul up his enormous eyelid. Now it was well-known that Balor's eye was a deadly weapon itself. Anyone he looked at died immediately. Lugh knew this perfectly well, so just before the eye was fully open, he swirled and twirled his catapult and let fly a magic stone which hit Balor so hard that he fell backwards, quite dead.

Then Lugh Long-Arm shrieked his battlecry, and joined by Morrigan Battle-Crow they and the Children of Danu drove the giants out of Eriu and down beneath the sea, where they stayed for ever.

The great red bowl of the sun sank behind a small rocky island as Coll steered the boat towards the black shadow of Eriu.

"I wonder if that's the entrance to Donn's kingdom under the sea," he murmured.

"I expect so," said Branwen. "It feels magical. Now, tell me the story."

✦ 25 ✦

Donn, Lord of the Dead

The time of Danu's children was passing, and soon the tall people of Mil came to Eriu on the wings of the west wind. Among them was a great king, Donn, son of Mil. His body was strong and his eyesight was keener than an eagle's. As his ship approached the shore at sunset, he climbed the mast to see what he could of this new land. The last of Danu's children were hidden behind rocks, and when they saw Donn's fierce face peering at them from so high up, they took fright and threw the magic spear of Finias at him. Down fell Donn in a blaze of red light, down into the very bottom of the sea. The people of Mil wept and

wailed, and ran ashore and fought Danu's children until they fled underground into the hills and green places of Eriu.

And Mil's chief bard, Amergin, declared that Donn should be Lord of the Dead, and that the people of Mil should go to his kingdom under the sea when their lives were over, where they would become young again for ever.

Now the magic spear of Finias had hurt Donn badly, so that he spent most of his time asleep in his undersea palace under Bull's Rock. The god Manannan sent nine beautiful sea-maidens to look after him, and each of them took turns to work in Donn's palace kitchen. There stood the huge cauldron of the sun. Every dawn the sun rose out of the bubbling, fiery cauldron into the sky towed by three red horsemen, and every night they drew it back down under the sea to be reborn. The maidens' job was to blow on the fires under the cauldron to keep it hot while the sun was away. Then the sun would never go out over Eriu.

Another dawn broke, and Coll sailed into the small harbour below the fort of Dealga. Four white swans glided over the sea towards him and surrounded the boat, hissing mournfully, and raising their wide white wings in greeting.

"Remember our story," came a whisper on the wind. "Look for Lir's protection in time of danger."

"Fionnula, Aodh, Conn and Fiachra," said Coll, bowing to them. "The children of Lir . . ."

✦ 26 ✦

The Children of Lir

In the time after the battle of Moytura, a new king ruled Eriu. But Lir, god of the ocean, was angry that he had not been chosen to sit on the throne. He stormed out of the king's palace at Tara, and stayed sulking in his fortress at Deadman's Hill. The king left him alone, and none of the other gods and goddesses would visit him. So Lir became very lonely, and he was lonelier still after the mother of his famous son Manannan died.

So when the king offered to find him a new wife, he agreed, and he chose Evva, daughter of the king of Aran. Soon they had four lovely children, three boys and a girl, called Conn, Fiachra, Aodh and Fionnula. Lir loved them all.

But Evva died having Conn and Fiachra, and so Lir married Ayfa her sister instead. Ayfa was a jealous woman, quite different from gentle Evva, and she was determined to get rid of the children and have Lir all to herself.

"Let me take the dear children to see the king," she said to Lir one day. "They should see the great palace at Tara, and meet their cousins." So Lir agreed.

Bump crunch crack went the carriage wheel as it broke. "Come, children," said Ayfa. "It's a hot day. Why don't you go for a swim in Lough Derravarragh while the wheel is mended?" The children stripped off their clothes and ran laughing into the cool waves. But as each of them did so, Ayfa touched them with a magic wand, and soon there were no children, just four white swans swimming on the water. Ayfa raised her arms and began to chant:

> *"Three hundred years on the waves of this Lough;*
> *Three hundred years on the waves of the sea,*
> *Three hundred years on Inish Glora isle*
> *Nine hundred years shall your punishment be.*
> *Till the Man of the North weds the Lady of South,*
> *Swans you shall be, except for your song.*
> *Lost to family, strangers to friends,*
> *Nine hundred years till your exile ends."*

When Ayfa had finished, she drove away, and all that was left behind was a sighing and a sobbing from the beaks of Lir's children.

Ayfa told lie upon clever lie about how the children had been killed by wild wolves when she returned to Lir's fortress. But Lir was suspicious, and he galloped off to look for them. When he got to Lough Derravarragh he heard a beautiful voice singing behind a rock.

"Fionnula!" he cried. "Is it you?" And then he wept as four swans swam slowly into sight, and sang to him of Ayfa's wickedness. At once he returned home, and bundled Ayfa into a big wicker basket. He dragged her before the king, who turned her into a blood red raven, and banished her to serve Morrigan, the goddess of war, for ever. Then Lir returned to the Lough, and for three hundred years he came to see them every single day. But at the end of that time, a huge wind blew up, and hurled the four swans up into the air and dropped them into the middle of the Irish Sea, and they knew they would never see their father again. Fionnula tried to shelter her brothers under her wings, but the cruel winds and waves blew them apart again and again, and they shivered and shook with the icy cold until they thought they would die of it. But Ayfa's evil spell would not allow them to die, and after another three hundred years they were blown to the island of Inish Glora, where they paddled ashore and made a home in a little lake.

There was a druid named Kemog living there, and the children of Lir sang to him every night, and in return he fed them with barley bread and milk from his goat.

Now, when the nine hundred years were nearly up, a warrior-prince came to Inish Glora from the North. "Wise Druid," he said, bowing to Kemog. "My wife-to-be has demanded that I bring her four enchanted white swans bound in silver chains before she will marry me. It came to me in a dream that you can tell me where I might find them." Then Kemog led him to the little lake, and there he found Fionnula, Aodh, Fiachra and Conn swimming and singing their sad song. They bowed their feathery necks meekly, and the prince fastened long silver chains between each pair. "Now follow me south," he cried, as he set sail.

So the children of Lir were there when a Man of the North wed a Lady of the South. As the bells pealed out in celebration, a rainbow mist drifted round the swans, and out of it stepped four beautiful children, dressed in white. And what happened to them after, no one can say.

As soon as Coll landed at the foot of Dun Dealga, on the shores of Eriu, a red mist sprang up around him, hiding the green hills. The violent sounds of a hurley game filled his ears, the clashing of stick and ball and the tramp of running feet coming nearer and nearer. But Coll remembered Broc's warning at the pool. He took out his harp and began to play a magical tune that Uath had taught him long ago. Silence fell, except for the baying of a great hound. "Who comes to Eriu?" it howled.

"Coll Hazel the Bard," said Coll, "and I seek Brehanna of the Golden Herds."

At once the mists parted, and Coll saw a gigantic warrior seated in a chariot drawn by two horses, one grey, one black. A shining cloud of mayflies danced round his head, and he wore a necklace of dogs' teeth. Branwen flew to perch on his shoulder.

"Who . . . who are you?" asked Coll. He felt strange, as if time was running both fast and slow, and as he looked about him the land shimmered oddly, as if it was not quite there.

"I am Cuchulain, little bard, sent by Lir from the Otherworld to help you past Brehanna's doorkeepers," he said. "Get in. I will tell you my story as we ride the road north to Emain Macha."

✦ 27 ✦

The Birth of Cuchulain, Hound of Cullen

Princess Dectera was dressed for her wedding to Sualtim of the Red Branch, when she heard the buzzing of a golden mayfly at the window. Dectera looked up, and the mayfly had turned into the most beautiful man she had ever seen. All brightness and fire he was, and soon Dectera found herself whirled around and about and away to a place where time ran faster than a racing horse, and the wine tasted of honey, and the golden man showed her magic and sang to her till she forgot Sualtim entirely.

But Sualtim and the men of the Red Branch did not forget Dectera. They searched and searched all over the kingdom, but there was no sign of her. They returned only just in time for harvest, but as soon as they got there, a cloud of pecking, squabbling birds flew down and started eating all the corn. The weary warriors chased the birds away for a day and a night, and then fell down exhausted on a high mound.

A white mist surrounded them, and they dreamt they were in a golden palace, where a golden warrior served them food and drink and gave them soft beds to lie on. In the morning they woke up, and to their surprise, there was Dectera, lying in the midst of them, with a baby boy in her arms.

"Lugh! Where are you?" she murmured as she awoke. And by that the men of the Red Branch knew that Dectera had been stolen by Lugh Long-Arm the sun god himself, and that her child was his son. She had named him Setanta.

Now Sualtim still loved Dectera, and she remembered how much she loved him, so he married her and brought Setanta up as his own. Setanta was good at everything from fighting to leaping to riding a horse. When he was six years old, he ran away from his mother, and went to visit his uncle, King Conor. On his way there, he met some older boys playing hurley.

"Let me play," he said. But the boys jeered at him and said he was too small.

"Just you wait," said Setanta. "I bet I can beat you all with one hand tied behind my back." And he did. King Conor was so impressed with his nephew that he invited him to dinner with his oldest friend, Cullen the smith. It was a great honour, for Cullen made the finest spears and swords in all Eriu.

"Be on time, boy," said King Conor. "Cullen lets his guard dog out after dark, and no one gets past him alive!" But Setanta was so exhausted from the hurley game that he fell asleep, and when he set off for Cullen's house it was dusk.

King Conor was inside, drinking and laughing and having such a good time that he forgot to tell Cullen that his nephew was coming to dinner. Darkness fell just as Setanta reached the gate, and as he put his hand on the latch, a fearsome barking exploded in his ear. Teeth the size of knives snapped near his nose, and claws like razors stretched towards his stomach.

Soon Setanta was fighting for his life. All he had with him was his hurley stick, and with it he beat off the huge dog until it lay down in the dust and died.

Trembling with fear, Setanta went in to confess to the king and Cullen what he had done. Cullen was very angry.

"You have destroyed the protection of my house, so you yourself shall be my hound for a year and a day and protect me until I can train up a new dog." And King Conor commanded Setanta never to eat dogmeat on pain of death, and said that he should have a new name in honour of his new job. The king called him Cuchulain, Cullen's Hound, and that was his name for ever afterwards.

At the doors to Emain Macha grew a great holly tree covered in berries, and at its foot sat three old women spinning their own hair on cowhorn spindles.

"Welcome, Coll Hazel," they said. "You must answer our riddle and defeat the guardians before you can go to Tara." Then they began to chant:

> I have been a mayfly's babe A destruction of wheat
> An iron man's dog I have been a rage of battle
> A crown of fiery blood A shining moon brow
> I have fought the eel goddess And the cow goddess
> And the crow goddess And they are all one
> Who is my father?

"Lugh Long-Arm," said Coll.

At once the ghosts of many fierce warriors rose up from the ground. Cuchulain drew his spear, Gae Bulga, and his hair stood on end and burst into flame at the tips. "Give me a battlesong, bard," he cried as he waded into the fight.

So Coll sang about the rage of Cuchulain, and as each ghost was defeated, it sank back into the ground. Soon there were none left.

"You have passed the test," said the old women to Coll, giving him a golden holly berry. "Brehanna's bowl awaits you at Tara."

✦ 28 ✦

The Rage of Cuchulain

The wind whistled and twirled around King Conor's palace of Emain Macha, seeking out secrets and lies. And soon it heard the voice of Cathbad the druid speaking a prophecy.

"The boy who takes up his first weapons and drives his first chariot today," said Cathbad, "shall be a wonder and a terror in all Eriu and tales of his high deeds shall be told for ever. But his life shall be as swift as that of a running hound, and his end shall be glorious." The wind whipped the words out of Cathbad's mouth, and whirled them straight into Cuchulain's ear. At once he leapt up from his game of hurley and ran to his uncle.

"I must have my weapons and my chariot today, your majesty," he said.

"Don't be ridiculous, you are only seven years old," said his uncle. But Cuchulain nagged and nagged, so Conor gave him two spears and a shield and a sword. When Cuchulain had finished testing them, they lay in splinters on the floor. It was the same with all the rest of the weapons in the palace. Nothing was strong enough for Cuchulain except the king's own weapons, so he gave Cuchulain those.

Then Cuchulain tried out all the chariots in the stableyard. Again, none was strong enough for Cuchulain, except for the king's own. King Conor sighed, and put the reins of his best horses into Cuchulain's hand.

"I suppose you'll want to go out and find an enemy to fight now," he said. "Though I don't know what your mother will say if you get yourself killed." Cuchulain was much too excited to listen, and he ordered his driver, Ibar, to drive northwards.

Ibar grumbled and muttered under his breath about having to drive such a little boy, but he didn't dare to offend the king's nephew. Soon they had crossed out of Ulster and were driving up a long hill, topped by a finger of stone which pointed to the sky. There was writing on the stone. *"The champion who reads this must fight the sons of Necht in single combat, or else be cursed."* Now the sons of Necht were fierce enemies of the men of Emain Macha, who had killed their father, and few could stand against them in battle. Cuchulain climbed down from the chariot.

"Is that where the sons of Necht live?" he asked Ibar, pointing at a castle across the plain below. Ibar said it was. "Then I shall send them a warning that I am coming to fight

them," said Cuchulain. And he lifted the huge stone up, and hurled it all the way to the field in front of the castle, where it stuck in the earth, quivering. Then Cuchulain made Ibar drive towards it.

"What did I do to deserve this?" complained Ibar. "You'll be killed in a trice, and King Conor will blame me."

As Cuchulain got out of the chariot, the three sons of Necht were waiting for him. "Who is this great warrior come to fight us," they sneered. "A little boy?" And they laughed till they fell down. Cuchulain felt a rage such as he had never felt before. His hair stood on end, and each hair blazed with fire. His face became ridged with stripes of green and yellow and blue. One eye popped out onto his cheek, and the other popped out of the back of his skull and a shining moon appeared on his forehead. From his head burst a great jet of black blood, and all his muscles turned themselves inside out. He was a terrifying sight. He drew his sword, leaping and twirling and roaring like a thunderstorm, and soon the three sons of Necht were lying headless on the ground. Cuchulain seized their heads as trophies, and growled at Ibar to drive him back to Emain Macha.

King Conor was keeping watch from the gatehouse. Soon he saw a cloud of fiery dust coming towards him. White swans flew above it, and the wild brown deer ran behind. Suddenly he heard a shout from Cathbad the druid. "Let the women bring three barrels of icy water out into the road, for if Cuchulain comes into Emain Macha in his battle rage, he will burn the palace." So all the women lined up outside the gates, and when Ibar had stopped the chariot, the women very carefully lifted Cuchulain down and plunged him into the first barrel. *Pop Crack* went the timbers in an explosion of steam. After

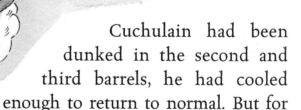

Cuchulain had been dunked in the second and third barrels, he had cooled enough to return to normal. But for ever afterwards, he had seven toes and fingers on each hand and foot, and seven pupils like jewels shone in each eye. He had a blue spot, a purple spot, a green spot, a yellow spot on each cheek, and fifty locks of bright-yellow hair ran from one ear to the other, like a cockscomb of pale gold.

"Let us have the Feast of the New Warrior," shouted King Conor. And all the people of Emain Macha cheered their new hero, Cuchulain.

As the chariot left Emain Macha by the royal road south, a huge brown bull bellowed from a nearby field.

"Did you ever hear the story of the time I defeated Queen Maeve of Connacht?" asked Cuchulain.

"Tell me how it was," said Coll.

And so Cuchlain told the story of the cattle raid of Cooley.

✦ 29 ✦

The Cattle Raid of Cooley

"Ailill," said Queen Maeve of Connaught, poking her husband in the ribs, "my fortune is just as big as yours, isn't it?" King Ailill sighed and turned over on his pillows. This conversation had been going on for days, and he was tired of it.

"There is only one way to solve this, my dear. We shall have to count everything we each own, and then we will have an answer to your question." So, for the next month, the royal household counted and scribbled until even the tiniest grain of corn and battered cooking pot was recorded.

And at last it was found that Maeve and Ailill had exactly the same fortune – except for one thing. Ailill owned the great bull Whitehorn, and Maeve had no beast to match him.

Maeve was furious. It seemed to her that life wouldn't be worth living until she had just such a bull of her own. So she sent her steward into the neighbouring kingdom of Ulster to borrow the Brown Bull of Cooley, who could have been Whitehorn's brother. But Dara, the bull's owner, said she couldn't have him.

"In that case," said Maeve to her warriors, "we will just have to steal him."

When Dara heard of Maeve's plan, he sent for help to King Conor of Ulster. But King Conor and all the men of the Red Branch had been struck down by a mysterious curse, which meant that they couldn't move from their beds. Only Cuchulain had escaped the curse, and he set off for the border with Connaught at once to defend Ulster all by himself. On the way he met a beautiful red-headed young woman, who offered him all her lands and cattle, if only he would stay with her. But Cuchulain was in too much of a hurry, and he refused her. At once the woman turned into a black raven with blood-red eyes.

"I am the Morrigan, and now you are my enemy," she croaked. "I shall come against you as an eel and a she-wolf and a hornless red cow – and you will die!" Cuchulain just laughed and waved his slingshot at her as he ran on. "I shall beat you every time!" he cried.

At the Ford of Thirst he waited for Maeve and her army. When they arrived, Cuchulain challenged a Connaught warrior to single combat every day from the last day of winter to the first day of spring, and every day a man fell to the rage of his thunderstorm fighting. The ford ran red with the blood of many fine warriors, and Cuchulain even had to fight his best friend, Ferdiad, and kill him, which he did with tears running down his face.

And then, when Cuchulain was tired and weak and wounded and sad, came Maeve's greatest warrior, Loch, and with him, under the waters of the ford, came the Morrigan eel. The eel wound itself around Cuchulain's ankles,

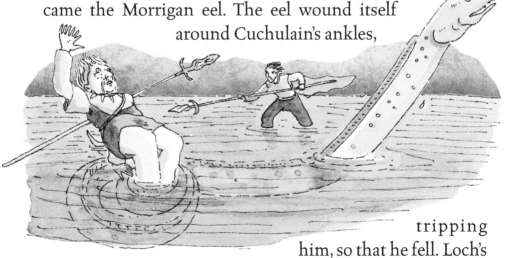

tripping him, so that he fell. Loch's spear pierced his side, and his blood stained the water. But Cuchulain got up and kicked the eel till its ribs broke.

Then the Morrigan came at him as a she-wolf, but he took out her eye with a stone. Last of all she came at him as a cow leading a thundering herd of red cattle, but Cuchulain whacked her with his sword and broke her leg, and she retreated, beaten as he had promised. Then he overcame Loch with his magic spear, the Gae Bolga, as darkness fell.

Just as Cuchulain fell down exhausted by his fire, too tired to eat or think or dress his wounds, a man appeared by his side in a blaze of golden light.

"I am your father, Lugh Long-Arm. Sleep, my son, while I heal your wounds, and I will fight in your place." So Cuchulain slept for three days, while his father fought the warriors of Connaught.

Now while Cuchulain was sleeping, Maeve had sent a band of cunning thieves to steal the Brown Bull of Cooley

134

from Ulster. As soon as he crossed the border into the strange land of Connaught, the Brown Bull bellowed aloud three times and ran to the top of Mount Cruachan. And Ailill's bull Whitehorn heard him and rushed across Connaught to attack him. For a whole day and a night all anyone could hear was the bellowing as the bulls rampaged over all Eriu. But at last the men of the Red Branch, now released from their curse and marching to help Cuchulain, saw the Brown Bull striding over Cruachan from the west with Whitehorn's skin hanging about his ears and horns in torn fragments.

So in the end neither Maeve nor Ailill had a bull, and Cuchulain and the men of the Red Branch defeated their army and chased it all the way back to Connaught.

An enormous crow flew overhead and landed on a tall stone in a nearby field. Branwen huddled into Coll's neck as a pair of burning red eyes glared at her. The crow cawed scornfully.

"This is Clochafarmore, where I must leave you," said Cuchulain, helping Coll down. "The Morrigan is calling me back to the past to my death fight, and you must brave the mortal world alone for a while." As he spoke, the red mist swirled about the stone, and again Coll heard sounds – this time of battle and slaughter.

"Quick, play your harp," croaked Branwen. "Or we will be dragged into the past too."

There was only one story to recall at that moment – the death of Cuchulain himself.

✦ 30 ✦

The Death of Cuchulain

The one-eyed hag daughters of Calatin hated Cuchulain because he had killed their father. For many years they travelled to lands near and far, learning magic spells and witchcraft so that they could get their revenge. When they came back to Eriu, they raised an army with Queen Maeve, and marched against him into Ulster.

Even though they had been forbidden to do so by King Conor, Cuchulain and his charioteer Laeg harnessed his magic horses Grey Macha and Black Sainglain, and drove off to fight Maeve and her army.

On the road they met the three daughters of Calatin, cooking dogmeat on a little fire of rowan twigs. Now Cuchulain had long before been forbidden by King Conor to even touch dogmeat.

"Eat with us, son of Lugh," they cackled. But Cuchulain refused. He knew they were up to no good.

"It's only because we haven't got a grand big hearth to cook on," they whispered. "He's too proud to eat by the roadside." So Cuchulain took a small morsel of dogmeat to be polite, but as it touched his mouth, all the strength went out of his left side, and he fell to his knees. He had broken King Conor's command. The daughters of Calatin shrieked in triumph and flew back to their troops in a whirling black cloud of crow feathers.

The sound of harps tinkled and chimed when Cuchulain got to the battlefield, and an enemy bard stepped out to meet him. "Give me your spear, Cuchulain, or I will curse you," ordered the bard.

"I cannot refuse you," said Cuchulain. "Take this." And as his battle rage came on him, he threw the spear so hard that it flew straight through the bard, and the nine warriors behind him too, not stopping until it was caught by his enemy Lugaid.

"Throw it back, Lugaid!" screeched the daughters of Calatin. "That spear is cursed to kill three kings." So Lugaid threw it at Cuchulain. But it hit Laeg, king of charioteers, and killed him instead. And that was one king.

Then a second bard stepped out. "Give me your spear, Cuchulain, or I will curse you," he said. And Cuchulain pulled it out of Laeg's body and answered as he had before. This time the spear went through the bard and eighteen warriors, and was caught by Erc.

"Throw it back, Erc," screamed the daughters of Calatin. So Erc threw the spear at Cuchulain. But it killed Grey Macha, king of Eriu's horses instead. And that was two kings.

A third bard stepped out. "Give me your spear, Cuchulain, or I will curse you," he said. So Cuchulain pulled it out of Grey Macha's heart and answered as he had before. This time the spear went through the bard and thirty-six warriors. Cuchulain rushed after it, leaping his thunder leap, with his hair like lightning streaming behind and his sword cut the enemy down like ripe corn. But Lugaid had caught his spear again, and this time he did not miss. It went right through Cuchulain from his front to his back. With the last of his strength Cuchulain tied himself to a tall grey pillar of stone, so that he would die standing up. Suddenly, a huge black raven with blood-red eyes landed on his shoulder. "I have come to see your death, king of heroes!" croaked the Morrigan.

But Cuchulain took no notice, and drew his sword for the last fight. As the sun died in a bloody red west, so Cuchulain's strength failed, and Lugaid cut off his head. The battlefield was dark and quiet, and all that could be heard was the triumphant croaking of the Morrigan and the crow crying of the daughters of Calatin. And never again in all Eriu was there a hero like Cuchulain, son of Lugh.

By now they were at the fairy broch, Brugh na Boyne. Coll sat down on top of a green mound surrounded by an ancient stone circle.

"Not sensible," cawed Branwen. "Don't go to sleep or the fairies will steal you."

But Coll was too tired to care. His eyes closed, and suddenly he was in the midst of a riotous feast.

"Greetings, Coll Hazel!" said a blue man. "And what are you doing in Lugh's palace?" For this was Lugh's home in the Otherworld.

"I need to get to Brehanna at Tara," said Coll. "And now I'm lost."

"Then you must tell me a story to make me laugh," said the blue man. "A story about me," he added, shaking a branch of silver bells.

So Coll told the story of the silver branch which brought happiness to Tara — at a price.

✦ 31 ✦

The Silver Branch

In all the land of Eriu there was never such a man for believing things as King Cormac. You could tell him any amount of old rubbish, and he would believe it. King Cormac had such a group of noisy farradiddlers and charlatans and plain old tricksters around him that the truth was rarer than gold in the palace of Tara.

One fine May day, on the feast of Beltane, King Cormac stepped up onto the ramparts of Tara, the royal palace, to get away from their squabble and chatter and arguing. As he listened to the song of the larks in the blue sky, he saw a blue man riding up to the gates with a bag on his shoulder.

"Ho! King Cormac!" shouted the blue man. "I have a wonder and a treasure in my bag. Do you want to see it?" King Cormac rushed down at once, and soon he was staring, spellbound, at a silver branch with three golden apples hanging from it.

The blue man shook it and the sound it made was so entrancing that all the tricksters stopped squabbling, and everyone in the palace felt so happy that any misery just melted away.

"Whatever you want, you shall have, but you must give me the silver branch," King Cormac begged.

"Well and so I will," said the blue man. "But you must give me three things in exchange, and I shall take the first when I come again." And with that he disappeared in a sea of mist, leaving a palace full of joy.

The next Beltane, the blue man appeared again. "I have come for my first reward," he said to King Cormac. "I shall take your daughter Elba."

King Cormac sighed. "A bargain is a bargain," he said, as the blue man disappeared into the mist with Elba. "And a king must keep his promises." But he had to ring the silver branch twice before the weeping and wailing stopped in Tara and everyone felt happy again.

The same thing happened the second year, but this time the blue man took Cormac's son Cairbry, and Cormac had to ring the silver branch three times before joy returned to Tara.

The third year the blue man returned and took Ethna, Cormac's beloved wife. This was too much, even for a king. So Cormac ran after him into the sea of mist, ringing the bells as he went. But now they brought him no joy at all. On and on he ran until he came out into another land entirely.

On the edge of a well surrounded by nine purple hazel trees sat the blue man feeding five silver salmon with nuts.

"I am Manannan Mac Lir," said the blue man, "Lord of the Ocean. In my palace, unlike yours, only truth is told. Come into my hall, and we shall see what we shall see." Manannan strode straight to the top table. "Prepare the feast!" he said, and suddenly a whole pig appeared on the spit in the huge fireplace. But however hard the spit boy turned the roast on the fire, it would not cook.

"This pig will never cook until a true tale is told," said the boy. And so Cormac told the true tale of how Elba and Cairbry and Ethna had been taken from him, and then the pig was cooked.

"Will you eat?" asked the blue man. But Cormac said he would never eat again until he could eat with his whole family. And that was true too. Just then a door opened, and Elba and Cairbry and Ethna came running in. What rejoicing there was! Then Manannan gave Cormac a golden cup and took the silver branch back.

"This will suit you better," he said. "For it breaks in three if a lie is told near it, and becomes whole again with the truth." When Cormac got home, he sent all the tricksters away, and Tara became the most honest place in Eriu. But Cormac never lost his love of a good story till the day he died.

"Stupid boy! I told him not to fall asleep!"

"Who knows how long he'll be in the Otherworld? Time runs differently there. He could stay with the fairies for a hundred years. Even ravens don't live that long."

"Where is he?"

"You've been gone for weeks," scolded Branwen, as Coll woke up, cold and damp, under the walls of Tara. "I've flown my wings off looking for you."

Coll shivered. "I've been telling stories to the Children of Danu," he said.

"Told you not to sleep on a fairy mound," said Branwen.

Just then they heard the sound of bells, and a flock of golden-fleeced sheep came out of the gates, followed by a golden-haired woman carrying a net. Coll held up his golden holly berry in greeting.

"Coll Hazel," said Brehanna. "I have been expecting you. Tonight is Imbolc, the time of New Ewes' Milk. Come and help me catch a salmon for the feast. You can tell me a fishing story while we walk."

"How about a story of a fish too good to eat?" said Coll. "Listen to the story of the Salmon of Wisdom!"

✦ 32 ✦

The Salmon of Wisdom

Finegas was a druid – but he was also a fisherman. And one fine day in May, he caught the biggest, finest salmon he had ever seen. "Surely this is one of the five Salmon of Wisdom, escaped from the Well of Knowledge,"

he said to himself. "I shall cook it and eat it, and then I shall be the wisest druid in all Eriu." But just as he had set the fish on the fire, he was called away on an urgent errand.

Now Finegas had an apprentice called Finn Mac Cool, a lazy, feckless, forgetful good-for-nothing of a boy, who dreamed of being a hero. But there was no one else around to tend the cookpot while he was gone. "Don't let the salmon burn, take it off the fire when it's done, and don't touch it, or eat any, because I shall know right away if you have," said Finegas to Finn Mac Cool, who nodded and smiled his usual sleepy smile.

An hour later, Finn Mac Cool woke up with a start from a dream of battle and glory. There was a strong scent of cooked fish. He leapt up, and snatched the cookpot off the fire. The lid fell to the ground with a clatter, and a waft of delicious salmon smell rose into the air. "I'd better make sure it's done," said Finn Mac Cool to himself. But he poked the salmon so hard that his thumb went right through into the pink, juicy flesh. "Ow! Ow!" he yelled, sticking his burnt thumb into his mouth. As he did so the salmon juice touched his lips, and all the salmon's wisdom went into him and not Finegas.

And for ever after, all Finn Mac Cool had to do was to stick the burnt thumb in his mouth, and he would know the answer to any question. Later on he became a hero, as he had dreamed, and he travelled all over Eriu and Alba with his band of warriors and his magic cow, Grey Shoulders.

Poor Finegas tried and tried to catch another Salmon of Wisdom. But he never succeeded.

The hall of Tara was still and dark with herb smoke as Brehanna drew a black veil over her hair. She poured the first ewes' milk of the year into a golden bowl at her feet, and dropped Coll's golden holly berry into it. The milk began to bubble and boil, and a white mist poured up and up, forming a radiant figure of light.

Inside Coll's head, a Goddess voice spoke. It sounded like thunder on a fine day. "Seek me at Llyn Tegid in Cymru on the eve of Beltane." Then it disappeared.

"Is that all?" asked Coll, disappointed. Brehanna sighed.

"Cerridwen is always mysterious," she said. "Goddesses always are. Now come and feast and let us tell stories of heroes. You must stay here for a while, till the spring storms are past, and then I will send a wind to blow you to Cymru."

Stories of heroes? A tale of Finn MacCool, of course, and the Burning of Tara.

✦ 33 ✦

The Burning of Tara

It was the feast of Shadows, and a drift of Otherworld music floated over the plain and through the doors and windows of the banqueting hall. The music was soft and soothing, and as soon as the High King and his court heard it, they fell asleep.

"ARRRRHHHH!" roared a vast voice. And galloping over the plain came the fiery warrior-monster Aillen. Round and round he galloped, breathing his burning Otherworld breath at the roof, and when he had finished the palace of Tara lay open to the rainy skies for the ninth year running.

"This must stop," said the High King. "Nine times this monster has burned my palace roof off. I need a hero." So he sent out messengers throughout Eriu. And on the day before the next Shadowfest, there came Finn Mac Cool, riding his black horse, and whistling a song of winter.

"Kill this monster, and you shall have your heart's desire," said the High King. So Finn agreed to try.

Now among the High King's warband, the Fianna, was an old man called Dog-Tooth. Just before the feast began, he ran up to the walls where Finn was keeping guard, and handed him a spear. "This is a magic spear," he said. "And the man who breathes its bitter smell will never sleep. I am too old to use it, but it will help you against Aillen." Sure enough, just as the High King had sat down, the sleepy music began, and silence settled over the banqueting hall. But Finn breathed in the bitter smell of his new spear, and stayed awake. Just as Aillen was starting to breathe fire, off the ramparts jumped Finn, right onto Aillen's back.

"Ho, monster!" he shouted. And he stabbed him right through the heart. As soon as Aillen was dead, the High King and all the court woke up.

"What is your heart's desire?" the High King asked Finn. Finn knew just what he wanted.

"Let me command your warband," he said. And so Finn commanded the Fianna from that day on.

On the Way to Cymru

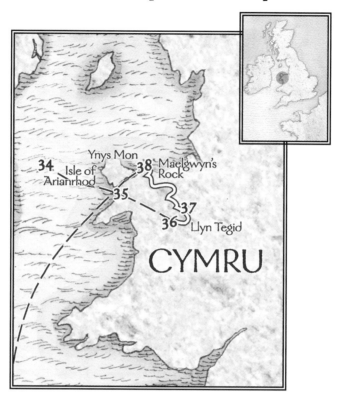

Coll and Branwen sailed east across the water to Wales, with Brehanna's gift of the west wind filling his sails. He was sorry to leave Eriu, but he had to get to Llyn Tegid by Beltane as the Goddess Cerridwen had commanded him.

"Tell me a story of Cymru," said Branwen. So Coll told her the story of Pryderi the Prince.

⊳ 34 ⊲

Pryderi the Prince

King Pwyll and Queen Rhiannon longed and longed for a child, and after many years they had a baby boy. They called him Pryderi, and he was the most precious thing in their lives. But one night, as he was asleep in his golden cradle, a huge green monster hand came down the chimney and stole the baby away.

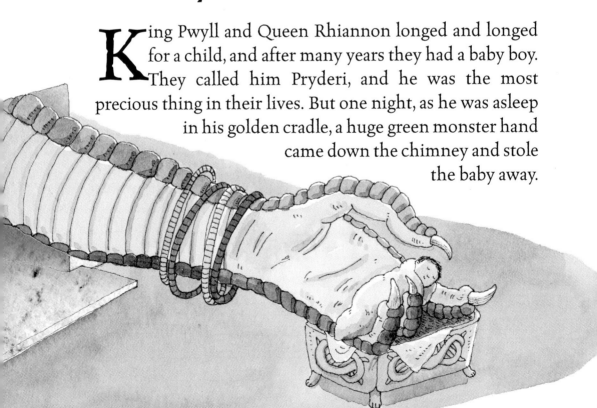

When Pryderi's nurse found the empty cradle, she was terrified. "What shall I do?" she moaned. And then a horrible idea came to her. She took some pig blood from the kitchen, crept into the sleeping queen's bedroom, and smeared it all round her mouth. "She's eaten the baby!" shrieked the nursemaid. And however much Queen Rhiannon protested that she hadn't, no one believed her, not even King Pwyll, and she was made to wear rags and carry visitors on her back across the castle courtyard as a punishment.

Now a long way from the castle lived a farmer called Teyrnon, whose pride and joy was his beautiful golden horses. But something was stealing his precious foals, and Teyrnon was determined to find out what it was that very night. As he sat up in the stable, holding an enormous sharp axe, there was a rattling at the shutters. Through the window came a huge green monster hand. It was holding a baby dressed in silk and velvet. The hand started to grope around the stable.

"Oh no you don't," said Teyrnon, and he cut the hand off. There was a wailing shriek, and the bleeding stump whipped up into the sky and vanished, leaving hand and baby behind. The baby started to cry.

"Well, and who are you then?" said Teyrnon, picking him up and taking him in to his wife. But no one knew who the baby was, so Teyrnon brought him up as his own son, and gave him a golden horse of his very own to play with. "I shall call you Pryderi," said Teyrnon.

But when Pryderi was four years old, the king's bard came riding through that part of the country, and with him came the tale of King Pwyll's dead son, and Queen Rhiannon's punishment.

"I am sure our Pryderi is the little prince," said Teyrnon's wife. "He's not dead at all. Go and tell the king at once." So Teyrnon and Pryderi mounted up on his golden horse and rode the long long way to the palace. At the gate they met Queen Rhiannon, thin and grey and tired.

"I must carry you to the king," she said. "Climb onto my back." But both Teyrnon and Pryderi refused. When the king heard Teyrnon's story, he wept with joy, and embraced his long lost son. Then he sent for Queen Rhiannon, and his apology to her was deeper than the bottomless sea. As for the lying nursemaid, she was set to sweeping out the cowbyre with a broom made of soft feathers. And as far as I know she is sweeping still.

The Isle of Arianrhod disappeared behind them in the spring dusk. The stars of Gwydion's Road laid a twinkling milky path across the sky above, and on the mainland an owl hooted.

"That reminds me of a story," said Coll, as he pulled the boat up the beach and settled down for the night, for an owl was at the end of the tale of Llew Steady Hand and Flowerblossom.

⊳ 35 ⊲

LLew Steady Hand and Flowerblossom

Llew Steady Hand wanted a wife. But when he was a boy, his mother Arianrhod had set a curse on him that he should never marry a human woman. "What shall I do?" he asked his uncle, Gwydion the magician.

"Leave it all to me," said Gwydion. Gwydion went to visit the wizard King Math and explained what his evil sister had done.

"What is the most beautiful thing in the world?" asked King Math.

"A flower," said Gwydion. So the two wizards took a cauldron and stirred oak blooms and broom blossom and the feathery yellow flowers of meadowsweet together, and sang spells over it for a day and a night. And at dawn a lovely woman stepped out of the cauldron, and they called her Flowerblossom, and gave her to Llew to be his wife.

Llew and Flowerblossom were happy together in the castle which King Math had given them. But one day when Llew was out, Flowerblossom heard the sound of hounds chasing a stag through the nearby forest, and she ran out to see the hunt. As soon as she saw Gronw Pebwr, Lord of Penllynn, at the head of his men, she fell in love with him, and he with her.

"We must get rid of Llew," said Gronw. "Then we can be together for ever." Now Llew could not be killed by any normal means. He had to be by a running river, under a roof of ferns; and he had to have one foot on the edge of a cauldron and one foot on the back of a deer. And he could only be wounded by a spear that had been made on Sundays. When Flowerblossom heard this, she set Gronw

to making the spear. It
took him a whole year.
Then she set a cauldron by
the river under a fern roof
and went to Llew.

"I have been thinking
and thinking," she said, "and I
just don't see how it is possible
to stand on a cauldron and a deer at the same time. Dearest
Llew, couldn't you show me, just once." So Llew went with
Flowerblossom to the place she had prepared, and got up
onto the cauldron edge.

"Just bring the deer a bit nearer," he said. "Now! See
how easy it is?" But as he spoke, Gronw jumped out from
behind a tree and stabbed him. Immediately Llew turned
into an eagle and flew away, screaming.

When King Math and Gwydion heard what had
happened, they were furious. As soon as they had found
Llew and healed him and turned him back into a man, they
took an army and set off after Flowerblossom, who had run
away to the mountains.

"Ha! Wretched woman!" cried
Gwydion when they had
caught up with her. "What I
have made I can unmake!
From now on you shall be
Owl, and all other birds
will attack you if you show
your face to the sun. You
shall be a sign of darkness and
ill-omen for ever." And as he struck
her with his wand, she flew away, screeching dismally.

As for Gronw, he went and hid. But Llew soon found
him by the river Cynvael, and stuck him with his own spear.
As the spear touched him, Gronw turned into a huge stone
with a hole through the middle. And there he stands on the
riverbank to this day.

Some weeks later, Coll and Branwen were lost in the damp Cymru fog when they met a small, bald fisherman with a coracle on his back. "I'm looking for Llyn Tegid," Coll said.

"Why, it's right here, boyo," said the fisherman. As he spoke, the sun came out and he pointed to an island in the middle of the lake. "That's where I live, with my wife. I think she's waiting for you," he said.

Coll's eyes widened. Could he mean Cerridwen? He didn't look at all like the sort of husband a goddess would have. "Could you take me out there?" he asked extra politely, just in case. For he knew all too well the tale of the Cauldron of Cerridwen and her power.

⊗ 36 ⊗

The Cauldron of Cerridwen

The goddess Cerridwen was tall and beautiful and mysterious as a starry night. She lived in the middle of Llyn Tegid with her husband, her daughter Creidwy and her son Avagdu. Now Creidwy looked like her mother, but Avagdu was uglier than an ogre's eyebrows.

159

"Poor child," said Cerridwen. "If he can't be handsome, then he shall be clever." And she took her magical cauldron, and set it to boil over the fire in her kitchen. She picked a little of this herb, a little of that flower, a scatter of berries and sprinkled in sunshine and moonlight, the song of a wren, and a dash of seafoam. Then she called her kitchen boy, Gwion. "You must stir this cauldron for a year and a day," she said. "And you must never let the fire go out, nor lick the spoon."

Gwion had no choice but to obey. Though his hand ached and his eyes drooped, he never stopped once. But on the very last day of his stirring, Cerridwen's white sow came running into the kitchen and bumped his stirring arm. Three drops of the precious liquid flew into the air, and *plop!* straight into Gwion's mouth.

Immediately, Gwion knew every secret there was to know. He could understand the birds and animals and insects and fish. "Quick!" grunted the pig as she heard footsteps. "Run away before Cerridwen catches you!" So Gwion changed himself into a hare and ran ran ran across the fields.

When Cerridwen saw the empty kitchen she roared
with rage and quick as light, she turned herself
into a greyhound and chase chase chased
after Gwion the hare.

As Gwion came to the edge
of the island, he turned
himself into a
salmon

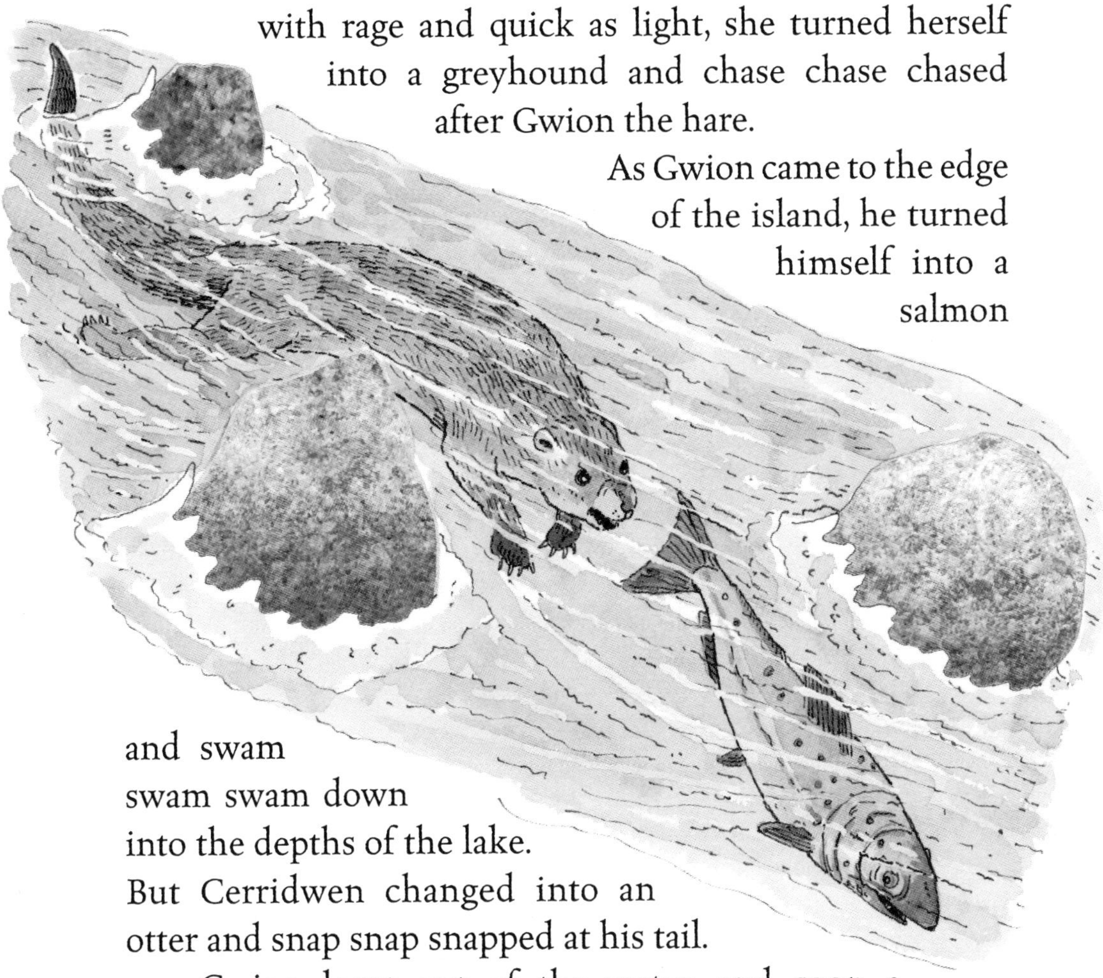

and swam
swam swam down
into the depths of the lake.
But Cerridwen changed into an
otter and snap snap snapped at his tail.

Gwion leapt out of the water, and soon a
blackbird was flit flit flitting over the water, with a hawk
dive dive diving after him.

By now Gwion was exhausted and confused, and as his
blackbird self reached the shore, it dropped down into the
long grass as a grain of corn. Soon a busy little hen had peck
peck pecked him up. "That's the end of him," said
Cerridwen, turning back into herself.

But it wasn't. Nine months later the corn in Cerridwen's stomach turned into a baby boy. Cerridwen was still very angry with Gwion, so she bundled him into a leather bag, and threw the baby into a river. "Get out of that!" she snorted.

And Gwion did. The leather bag washed into a salmon weir on Beltane Eve, and was found by Prince Elphin.

"What a lucky thing," said the prince when he saw the baby. And when the baby answered back and told him his story, Elphin was even more amazed. "I shall bring you up to be my bard," said Prince Elphin. "And I shall call you Taliesin Shining-Brow. I can see we are going to have adventures together." And so they did.

"Welcome, bard," said the goddess to Coll in a thundery voice he recognized as they pulled up on the island. "You have found me on Beltane Eve, and the fires are lit. Come and look into the flames."

As Coll stared, the flames caught his eyes, and drew him in, and his mind fell into a sea of dark. He heard the song of a blackbird, the roar of a stag, the hoot of an owl, the screech of an eagle – and over it all the thunder voice of Cerridwen the goddess, whispering the ancient story of Mabon and the Oldest Creatures.

"I will send you a guide at Maelgwyn's Rock," she said as the vision faded. And into his mind swam an ancient salmon, no longer silver, but black as night with age.

☙ 37 ❧

Mabon and the Oldest Creatures

In a time before time began, lived Modron and her husband Euron. And they were the very first of their kind, and their son Mabon was the very first child. But in the thirteenth month, when a blue moon shone over the land, Mabon was stolen away.

And so age upon age passed until Culhwch, nephew to King Arthur Pendragon, went with Cei and Bedwyr to look for him.

Culhwch was in love with Olwen, daughter to the giant Ysbaddaden. But the giant refused to let him marry her until Mabon was returned to the world.

Culhwch, Cei and Bedwyr asked in cottages and castles, farms and fortresses, caves and keeps, but no one had even heard of Mabon. So they went to Merlin the magician. "Try the Blackbird of Cilgwri," said Merlin. So they went to find her.

The Blackbird of Cilgwri lived behind the forge of Govannon the Smith. But when Culhwch asked if she had seen Mabon, she shook her head.

"I have sharpened my beak on Govannon's anvil till it is worn away to a nub of metal. But in all my long years, I have never heard of Mabon. You must try the Stag of Rhedynfre. He is older than me." So they went to find him.

The Stag of Rhedynfre lived in a glade in the forest of Ty Canol. But when he heard Culhwch's question, he shook his antlers. "When this oak tree was a sapling I came here, and now it is a worn-away stump of wood. But in all my long years I have never heard of Mabon. You must try the Owl of Cwm Cawlwyd. She is older than me." So they went to find her.

The Owl of Cwm Cawlwyd lived in a dark, gloomy valley. But she could not answer Culhwch's question either. "Two forests have grown and died here since I was born. But in all my long years I have never heard of Mabon. You must try the Eagle of Gwernabwy. He is older than me." So they went to find him.

The Eagle of Gwernabwy lived on top of a crag in the mountains. But when Culhwch asked if he had seen Mabon, he had not. "When I first came to this rock, it was so high I could peck the moon. But now the moon is far away and my nest is near the earth. You must find the Salmon of Llyn Llew. He is the oldest of us all." So they went to find him.

The Salmon of Llyn Llew blew bubbles when he heard Culhwch's question. "I have swum all the rivers of this land, and there is a spot behind the stones of Caer Loyw where a voice has sung of freedom since time began. I will take you there." So Culhwch and Cei and Bedwr climbed onto the Salmon's back, and sure enough when they reached Caer Loyw, behind the stones they heard a sweet, pure voice raised in a sad song of loss and loneliness.

"Call him," said the Salmon. So Culhwch, Cei and Bedwyr shouted out as loud as they could. As soon as the stones of that place heard Mabon's name, they crumbled to dust and Mabon was free at last.

Culhwch and Olwen were married soon after, and Mabon sang at their wedding – a song of bliss and delight to make the stars joyful.

Then Coll awoke, no longer by Llyn Tegid, but by a sea pool under Maelgwyn's Rock, with the sound of waves in his ears. His boat was drawn up on the sand beside him and a large fishy eye was looking at him from the water.

"Follow me," said the salmon, as he led them on southwards, and the coast of Cymru sped by.

"Do you know where we're going?" asked Branwen.

"No," said Coll. "But Ollach did say to take the paths we are shown, however strange. We'd better follow Cerridwen's guide. Remember what happened to Taliesin."

Just to remind them both, Coll told the story of the Holly Whip.

⊳ 38 ⊲

The Holly Whip

"**M**y thirteen-year-old bard is the greatest in Gwynedd," said Prince Elphin to King Maelgwyn. Now, the king was a vain man, who couldn't bear anyone to beat him. So he threw Prince Elphin in prison until he could prove his boast.

Taliesin Shining-Brow was skimming and skating over the thick winter ice, when he saw a picture of what had happened to Elphin in the frozen water. Immediately he rode to Maelgwyn's castle to save his master.

"I am Prince Elphin's chief primary bard," he said to the king. "And I challenge your bards to a contest."

"Pah!" snorted King Maelgwyn. "My bards have trained for twenty years. You don't have a chance." But Taliesin wiggled his fingers, and when Maelgwyn's bards came to sing, all that came out of their mouths was *blerm blerm blerm*. The king was furious.

"My turn!" said Taliesin. And as he started to sing, a hurricane whirled round Elphin's prison and shook it right down. Then he sang another song which snapped Elphin's chains. King Maelgwyn was frightened, but he wasn't going to give in.

"Your bard may be good, but my horses are faster than anyone's," he boasted to Elphin. "If you can't win a race with me you'll both go to prison."

Taliesin nudged his master. "I know how you can beat him," he whispered. So a race was arranged for the very next day.

When Taliesin came in riding an old grey mare with wobbly legs, King Maelgwyn rubbed his hands with glee.

"Let the race begin," he cried, and they were off. As each of Maelgwyn's fiery horses passed Taliesin, he tapped it on the rump with a burnt holly twig, and then dropped the twig on the ground. When all the horses were past, he dropped his cap. Then he ambled on up the course.

Soon the king's horses were racing back towards him and the finish line. But as each horse came to the twig which had tapped it, it reared up on its hind legs and started to dance. Taliesin and the grey mare ambled back down the course, and won the race. King Maelgwn had no choice but to let Prince Elphin and Taliesin go.

"Psst!" said Taliesin to Elphin on the way home. "Dig where I dropped my cap." So the prince dug a big hole, and lo and behold, there was a chest full of gold and jewels.

"Pulling you out of that weir was the best thing I ever did!" said Elphin. Taliesin just smiled.

Stories of Armorica

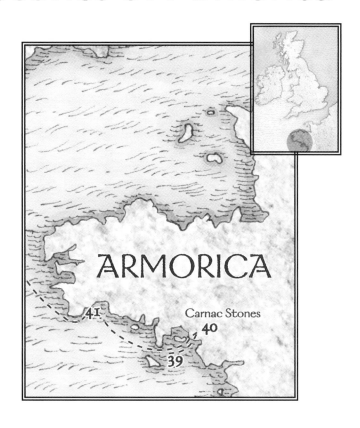

A fishy nose poked out of the waves beside the boat as they glided along the Armorican coast and into the bay of Carnac. It had been a long journey down the whole land of Dunein, past Kernow, and across the sea.

"The guardian of the dunes will find you soon. Give him this," said the salmon, flipping a silver scale into Coll's lap. "At the Midsummer moon he will show you the next step on your path." As he disappeared, a tiny green boat came up from the very bottom of the sea, rowed by a little old man, all in black.

"Ahhhhh!" he said, as Coll handed him the salmon's token. "So you are the one the mermaids bring news of. I am Yann-An-Odd. Come with me and I will teach you many secrets!"

◍ 39 ◍

Yann-An-Odd, Lord of the Dunes

"Hush," say the fishermen in their boats at dusk, "hurry!" And they sail swift and sure for the safety of the harbour and home. For far out in the dark and the drift of the waves comes a howling cry.

"I-ooou! I-ooou! I-ooou!" it goes, eerie and shrill as a seagull, a lonely, lost sound. And sometimes a sailor will sigh and stare, and turn his tiller for the open ocean, hearing words which draw him on, on, to the wrecking rocks and down into the deep. And there he will join Yann-An-Odd, Lord of the Dunes, in his house made of bones and sea-wrack and shell, surrounded by whispering ghosts and mermaids, who feast on silver pilchards and rainbow mackerel stolen from the nets above.

But at other times a sailor far out on the waves, lost and helpless in a storm, will hear in that cry a sound of hope and comfort, and he will see a green glow ahead. And an old man, sometimes giant, sometimes dwarf, but always dressed in black, will row in front of him and guide him safe to shore by the light of his shadowy lantern.

It all depends, say the fishermen, on whether the Lord of the Dunes is in a good mood or not.

A green glow surrounded the little man, and the rising Midsummer moon cast a giant's shadow behind him. He opened his mouth, and an unearthly shriek curled round the magic stones of Carnac, demanding an answer from the spirits. Coll held his breath as Branwen dug her claws into his shoulder. Suddenly, the biggest stone fell over and cracked open. A ghostly figure rose up.

"At Lugnasadh, seek the Merlin in the twisted wood," it said in a faint, grey voice, "and he will show you the way to the hill you seek."

"Another long journey," said Branwen crossly, as they lay down to sleep at moonset. "Tell me a Merlin story, or I'll peck you."

◑ 40 ◑

Merlin and the Young Magician

"Show me again!" cried Gwennolaik. So Josselin threw the rose petals up in the air, and pointed at them with his wand. "Arion!" he cried, and at once a flutter of pink butterflies surrounded the princess. She clapped her hands and kissed him.

"I shall tell my father that I will marry no one but you, Josselin," she said. But King Kado had other ideas.

"My daughter can't marry a young whippersnapper magician just like that," he said to his chamberlain. "I shall have to get rid of him. But how shall I do it without upsetting Gwennolaik?"

"A quest is usual, your majesty," said the chamberlain.

"Ha!" said the king. "I shall send him to steal Merlin's ring and harp. He'll never succeed, and if he does, Merlin will be so angry that he will come and turn him into a toad for ever. And Gwennolaik hates toads."

Now Josselin was a lot cleverer than the king thought he was, and he knew just what to do. For six days and nights Josselin battled through six magic woods – ash and birch, alder and rowan, apple and hazel – and on the afternoon of the seventh day he entered an oak wood. Right in the middle of the oak wood was a huge tree, and hanging from it was a golden mistletoe branch covered with thirty tiny, round golden bells. Josselin cut the branch and caught it in his cloak as it fell.

Then he turned himself into an eagle and flew off to the cave where Merlin lived and hid himself outside. As dusk approached, he took the branch and started to wave it from side to side. A gentle tinkling filled the air.

There was a loud yawn from inside the cave, and then snoring. Still waving the bells, Josselin crept into the cave and saw Merlin asleep on the floor. His harp was on the table and his ring was on his finger. Very gently, never letting the bells stop, Josselin put them both into his bag and tiptoed out. He turned himself into an eagle again and flew straight back to the palace, where King Kado was not at all delighted to see him.

"Blast!" he whispered to his chamberlain as Josselin walked towards him with a golden harp and a silver ring. "Now I shall have to send for Merlin." But as he spoke, there was a large green flash and a bang, and Merlin appeared in the throne room.

"Bless me," he said, sneezing and blinking. "And where is the clever young man who has relieved me of my most precious possessions? I should like to congratulate him. Never has such a thing happened in a thousand years." After that, there was really nothing King Kado could do but congratulate Josselin and give him his blessing. And two days later Josselin and Gwennolaik were married by Merlin himself. They had four sons who were all magicians. But none of them ever managed to catch Merlin napping ever again.

The enormous fleet of long-oared ships with their beaked prows passed the western tip of Armorica, just as Coll's boat shot into a hiding place among the rocks. Their sails were painted blood-red by the sunset.

"Raiders!" said Coll. "More than have ever come before. We shall have to be very careful on the way back to Kernow." Just then a rattle of stones tumbled down the cliff behind them. Branwen flapped nervously.

"Calm down," said Coll. "Anyone would think you'd heard old Ankou the Herald of Death."

"How do you know I didn't?" said Branwen, gloomily, but he listened to Coll's story all the same.

◑ 41 ◑

Ankou the Herald of Death

Brezonek was a curious boy, nose into this, nose into that. "What, where, why, how?" he asked his mother fifty times a day, until she was driven mad by his chatter, and bundled him out of the house.

"I'd have more peace rattling along with the pebbles in Ankou's old cart at next full moon than I get with all these questions," she shouted. But all that did was to start Brezonek off again.

"Who is Ankou? Where does he live? Why does he have pebbles in his rattly cart? When can I meet him? How do you know him?" The kitchen door slammed and Brezonek was left by himself in the muddy yard with the clucky chickens who were no good at all to an inquisitive lad. Over and over the questions turned in his head, until he couldn't stand it any more.

"I shall hide by the road at next full moon and see if I can find out who this Ankou is," he said to himself. And so he did.

Brezonek waited and waited, getting colder and sleepier by the minute, until he heard a rattling and a clattering coming along the road in the moonlight. His eyes grew round as he saw a skinny, scrawny horse, followed by a fat, glossy horse pulling a long, low cart driven by a tall man with a large black felt hat pulled down over his eyes and a large scythe by his side.

"Ankou!" he whispered. The carriage stopped immediately.

"Yes," said a creaky, bony sort of voice. "I am Ankou. My cart is full of the rattle of pebbles, but soon it will be full of the silence of souls when I collect my Master's harvest."

"W-w-who is your Master?" stammered Brezonek.

"Death," said Ankou. Brezonek turned and ran home as fast as his shaking legs would carry him. And from that day on he never asked another question.

Through Kernow

Two small heads peered over the rocks at Lulynn as they landed near the tip of Kernow. "What are you doing?" asked a boy and a girl, as Coll covered his boat with seaweed.

"Nosy children," squawked Branwen. But Coll looked up and smiled.

"I'm going on a long journey, and I won't need my boat any more. Will you look after it for me?"

"Ooh, yes!" they said. Then they saw Coll's harp. "Are you a bard?" they squeaked.

"I am," said Coll. "And I'll tell you a tale if you give me a bit of bread and ale."

So Coll told them the story of the Tolcarne Troll as he munched.

⌘ 42 ⌘

The Tolcarne Troll

I n a cave in the rocks, just where the blue sea meets the sky, lived a wise old troll. He came from a faraway country where enchantments were as common as rain in winter. But one day, when he was out fishing for mackerel, a great storm had driven his little boat all the way to Cornwall, and there he had chosen to stay. "This land has magic in its bones," he said.

But after many long years, the troll began to miss his own country, and longed to see what was happening there. So he gathered sand from the beach, and tin and gold from the earth, and he made himself an enchanted mirror that showed him things both near and far, true and false, things past, and things still to come. Now near his cave lived a nosy little girl called Zenna. One morning, as she was out on the cliffs searching for mushrooms, she heard a creaky little voice singing:

183

Kermennor, Kermannor, Trevennick, Tregerth,
Show me, oh show me the land of my birth.

But when she crept down the narrow path to the beach, there was no one there. The same thing happened the next day and the next. Zenna was determined to find out who was singing, so she went to her grandfather. "Ash and oak and thorn bring the fairy folk to light," said her grandfather. "But you be careful. You might get more than you bargain for."

At dawn, Zenna took a leaf of ash and oak and thorn, and when the singing started, she held them up, and said, "Come out, come out, whoever you are." And right then and there, a little old troll in a red leather jerkin popped out of nowhere, holding a shiny golden mirror. "Oh, how pretty," said Zenna, and she rushed to look in it. How she squealed when, instead of herself, she saw a pig with a long nose, dressed in the very clothes she was wearing that day.

"That," said the troll, "will teach you to be nosy." And he and his mirror vanished into thin air. As for Zenna, she never poked her nose into other people's business again.

Coll stood at the edge of the forest and looked out at the Mount of Lannvighal. The tide was high, and the waves lapped at the green stone.

"Do you know how that got there," he asked Branwen.

"Looks like giant's work," she said.

"What a clever raven you are," said Coll. "Indeed it is. Let me tell you the story of the Giant who killed his wife by mistake!"

⌘ 43 ⌘

The Giant's Wife

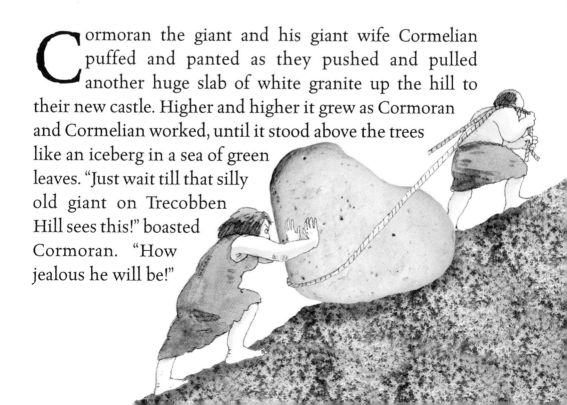

Cormoran the giant and his giant wife Cormelian puffed and panted as they pushed and pulled another huge slab of white granite up the hill to their new castle. Higher and higher it grew as Cormoran and Cormelian worked, until it stood above the trees like an iceberg in a sea of green leaves. "Just wait till that silly old giant on Trecobben Hill sees this!" boasted Cormoran. "How jealous he will be!"

At midday, Cormelian gave Cormoran a large slab of bread and onion, and a barrel of ale to drink. This made him sleepy, so he lay down under an oak tree.

"Carry on the work while I have a nap," he told his wife.

"Lazy, good-for-nothing giant," muttered Cormelian crossly. "Why should I fetch your fancy white granite from miles away, when there's perfectly good greenstone just next door?" The more she thought about it, the crosser she got. So she dug out a large piece of greenstone, put it in her apron and carried it up to the top of the wall. Just then Cormoran woke up. What a roar he let out when he saw what Cormelian was doing. Round and round the wall he chased her, and when he caught up with her he kicked her so hard in the bottom that she flew right over the trees and landed *splash!* in the sea. She was so heavy that the waves overflowed, and ran right up to Cormoran's castle, where they lap at the walls to this very day. As for the greenstone in Cormelian's apron, it soared straight up into the sky and landed *plop!* on top of Cormoran, killing him stone dead. And serve him right.

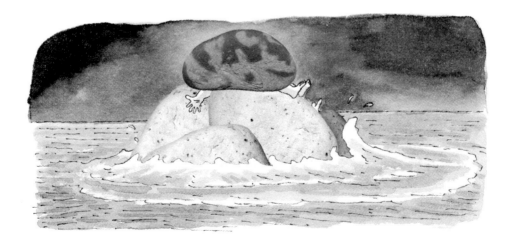

Coll trudged across Kernow, with the summer heat beating down on his head as he walked along dusty tracks, making his feet sore. Branwen soared in the cool breezes above the gorsy hills where only wild ponies lived. Suddenly she dived, squawking an alarm.

"Raiders! I see raiders behind us!" Coll looked behind to where a column of black smoke rose in the still air.

"We'd better hide," he said, making for a huge square rock. "We'll go on at nightfall."

"Tell me another giant story," said Branwen. "It'll make us both brave."

"I'll tell you the story of the good giant of Carn Galva," promised Coll.

⌘ 44 ⌘

The Giant of Carn Galva

The giant of Carn Galva loved to play. He would spend all day piling up the square rocks round his home into weird and wonderful shapes, and then he would whoop and whistle with joy as he kicked them down again.

187

Every night as the sun sank into the farthest west, he rocked himself to sleep on the big seesaw he had made, while seagulls swooped and swirled round his head.

Now there was a young man called Marec, who often walked up to Carn Galva from the nearby village to play with the giant, and keep him from getting lonely.

"Ho! Giant!" he called, as he ran up the rocks one fine morning. "Today is a day for hide-and-seek!" So Marec and the giant took it in turns to hide, and when it was Marec's turn to seek he often had to pretend not to see the giant, because he was so big and couldn't squeeze into small places.

"Where on earth can he be?" he said, looking up and down and everywhere but at the giant. And the giant would

spring up and cry, "Here I am!" and laugh and laugh until the tears ran down his huge red cheeks.

As dusk fell, the giant said goodbye to his friend. "I shall see 'ee again tomorrow," he said, patting Marec on the head with his enormous hand. But oh dear! His giant fingers went right through Marec's skull, and poor Marec fell down quite dead. How the giant cried and wailed, and tried to plug up the finger-holes with pastry. But it was no good, Marec was gone for ever.

The giant of Carn Galva was so sad and sorry that he never played any more after that. He sat so long and so still at the mouth of his cave that his body shrank and withered and turned to stone. And the seagulls nested on him, and the moss grew on him, and for all I know he is sitting there still.

The squawking of ravens filled the summer air as Coll walked along a streambed into Dartmoor. The moor stretched for miles around him, but just ahead a patch of shimmering mist lay over a small wood.

"What are they saying?" Coll asked Branwen.

"They talk of the twisted wood and the mystery within. They say that only one who has been to the Otherworld already can enter." A note of alarm entered her voice. "They say that the raiders are near."

Just then a striped head peered out of the bushes. "I am Biter," said the badger. "Come quickly. I will lead you to the Merlin's nest."

Coll hurried after the badger. "Biter must be the one of the animals who helped King Arthur pull out the sword in the stone," he muttered to Branwen.

"Tell me the story later," she croaked, flapping to keep up.

✥ 45 ✥

Merlin and the Sword in the Stone

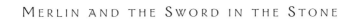

Merlin had summoned Art from his bed at dawn. "Where are we going?" he yawned. But Merlin only shook his head mysteriously and beckoned him on. Now Art sat against a willow tree and trailed one toe in the water. He watched as Merlin stumped over to the river's edge, and thumped his staff on the ground three times.

"Ahem!" said Merlin, clearing his throat. "Come Digger, come Biter, come Mover, come Fighter, come Strongwing and Stubborn and Hardgrip and Nighteye," chanted Merlin to earth underneath and sky above and deep water flowing.

And so they came, mole and badger, ant and bear, eagle and ox and pike and owl, gathering round the wizard in a tight circle of fur and feeler, feather and fin. He waved his staff at Art. "Come here, boy," he said. So Art came, edging into the circle between the soft fur of the mole and the grinning chin of the pike on the riverbank. "Now," said Merlin, "each of my friends has something useful to teach you, so look into Fighter's eyes, and we'll begin.

Art looked deep into the bear's eyes and felt himself falling. His whole self felt as if it was changing – shifting and flickering from shape to shape until he was filled with the strength and power and knowledge of every animal, bird, fish and insect in the circle. Then everything went dark and he knew nothing else.

Afterwards, Merlin picked Art up and carried him through the forest and back to the camp where the British warriors were gathered for the choosing of their new king, and put him to bed. Then he disappeared.

Art woke with a start as a toe thumped into his blankets.

"So this is where you are, you lazy toad," said Cei, his foster brother. "I've been looking for you everywhere. I need you to take my sword for sharpening. Hurry up and bring it back here!"

Art took the heavy sword and set off towards the forge, where the sharpening was soon done. But on the way back he stumbled on a clump of reeds beside the river, and the sword flew into the air. It landed with a splash, sinking in the swift current, and was gone without a trace.

"Oh no!" groaned Art into the mud. He knew he was in the biggest trouble of his life.

But as he trudged back towards the tent where Cei was waiting, a patch of pearly mist mysteriously appeared in his path. There in the middle of it, surrounded by an oak grove, stood a huge stone with a magnificent sword stuck right through it's centre. "Maybe no one will notice if I take that sword for Cei," said Art to himself.

There were some runes on the stone, but Art was in such a hurry that he didn't bother to read them. He climbed up and began to pull. The sword didn't move. Art pulled harder, till all his muscles creaked. The sword still didn't move. A small ant voice came from beside his left foot.

"Remember my strength," said Mover. A flap of wings sounded above him.

"Remember how to hold on," said Strongwing and Nighteye.

"Put some power into it," said the voices of Digger and Biter and Stubborn and Hardgrip and Fighter. So Art closed his eyes and remembered his lessons. Then he pulled again from his heart. The sword came away from the stone as easily as if it were melted butter. Art opened his eyes.

Around the stone Digger, Biter, Mover, Fighter, Strongwing, Stubborn, Hardgrip and Nighteye were saluting him.

"All hail Arthur, King that Is and King that Shall Be," they said.

The mist parted like a curtain as Coll stepped into the wood. Huge grey boulders lay scattered among the moss-covered trees.

"Play your harp," growled Biter. So Coll ran his fingers over the strings, and out came a tune he had never heard before. Suddenly, between the two biggest boulders, a crystal door appeared. As the music went on, it melted away, to reveal a dark cave entrance. Still playing, Coll bent his head and entered, Branwen on his shoulder.

There lay the Merlin, long grey beard tangled like the moss outside. He opened his eyes and sat up.

"Is Nimue's spell broken at last?" he asked sleepily. Coll put down his harp.

"It is, my lord Merlin."

"Then we must tread the secret paths of the Otherworld to Avalon together, and I will tell you of her as we go."

✿ 46 ✿

Merlin and the Fairy Enchantress

Merlin peered into the ancient crystal. Dark clouds raced across it, and a red dragon battled a white dragon in the skies, while below men fought under King Arthur's flag. "Always the same vision," he muttered. "But I cannot see any further into the future to see who wins. And I am so tired." He yawned and stretched and went into the sunshine.

Outside the cave, the little fountain shimmered in the sunlight as Merlin bent to drink. Suddenly the water shimmered with rainbows, and through the spray he saw a beautiful fairy girl walking out of the oak trees towards him. She had a crown of flowers on her head, and she carried a staff wound round with roses.

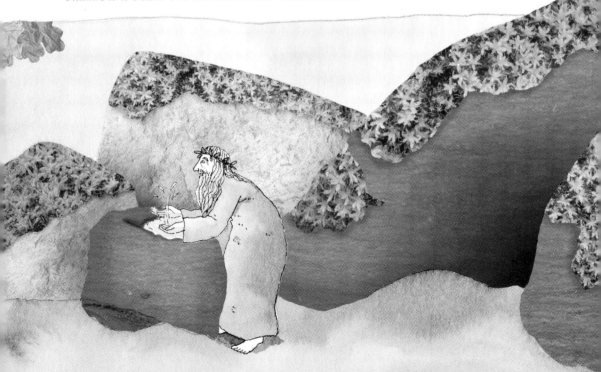

"I am Nimue," she said, looking deep into his eyes. And from that moment on, Merlin forgot all about his duty to King Arthur and the land and fell down into a deep enchanted sleep.

Nimue laid him on a soft bed of ferns and tucked furs around him. She took the crystal to the entrance of the cave and tapped it with her staff. At once it grew to fill the whole door, and the cave shimmered and sparkled with light.

"Sleep well, my lord Merlin," whispered Nimue. "King Arthur and his Companions must meet their fates without you, as the old prophecies foretell. But I will wake you when their time is over. It is not for ever."

As she walked away, the oak trees closed in behind her and became tangled and twisted together. They grew matted beards of grey moss, and their roots scrambled over the earth, and bent themselves into knots around the stones, until Merlin's cave was hidden completely, and passed out of all knowledge but that of the fairies.

Time did not exist on the Otherworld roads but as Coll walked, Merlin told all the tales of King Arthur but two. It was late October when they scrambled out of a badger's sett at dusk, onto a long hill overlooking a watery plain. Flames and the sound of swords were everywhere as the Viking raiders swept over the land.

Merlin swore. "I have been asleep too long. The Otherworld magic has tricked my feet and brought us to the wrong place. This spot is what remains of Camelot, where Arthur rode out to battle with his great sword, Caliburn. We must creep down onto the plain in the darkest part of the night, and hope that we aren't caught. The magic protecting the Treasures is very weak now, and the raiders will find them if we don't get there tomorrow."

"Tell me about the Lady of the Lake again," cawed Branwen. "I like that one."

"Be quiet, wretched raven," whispered Merlin. But he told the story anyway.

❋ 47 ❋

Merlin and the Lady of the Lake

King Arthur's sword, Caliburn, was dented and pitted from the blood of the green giant he had just killed. He wiped it carefully on the grass, and slid it into his belt.

"Why won't it stay in a scabbard?" he asked Merlin.

Merlin sighed. "You can't just put a magic sword in any old scabbard," said the wizard. "It has to be the right one."

Just then, a wren landed on his shoulder and peeped and cheeped into his ear. "Aha!" said Merlin mysteriously as he listened. "Come on, Arthur," he said over his shoulder as he turned and walked out of the forest. So Arthur followed, grumbling.

"You never answer my questions properly," he complained.

"Hush!" said Merlin.

Up hills and down valleys they went, until at dusk they reached a silver lake, whose waters stretched as far as the eye could see.

"Throw Caliburn into the lake," said Merlin. And he sounded so fierce and stern that Arthur lifted his arm and hurled the sword far out into the middle. The silver waters closed over it and it sank without a trace.

"Now we wait," said Merlin. And for once Arthur didn't ask questions, but sat peacefully. Soon he sank into a doze and dreamed of an underwater palace and a beautiful Lady sitting in a rose-pink room, sewing a long tube of gold and silver and jewels. When he woke at dawn, the sun was rising in the east, and a golden path stretched right to the lake's edge. "There is your way," whispered Merlin. So Arthur got up and stepped onto it. It was quite solid under his feet, and as he walked forward, he saw another marvel. A slender white arm had risen from the water, and it was holding a sword aloft. A sword with two familiar serpents on the hilt.

"Caliburn!" cried Arthur. But then he stopped. There was something different. The blade was now covered with a magnificent scabbard, set with gold and silver and jewels. As Arthur stretched out his hand to take the sword, he heard the voice of the Lady of the Lake. Soft and gentle it was, but there was steel in it too.

"Use my sword well, Arthur, until it is time to return it to me. And wear the scabbard always. It will stop you bleeding if you are wounded." And with that, the sword blazed up brightly in Arthur's hand, and he found himself back on the shore. The lake was silver and still again, and the arm had disappeared.

"Farewell!" called a voice from deep under the water. "Remember, we will meet again!" And then there was silence.

Merlin, Coll and Branwen dodged and crept their way around the force of warriors destroying the village and everything around. As dawn broke, they reached the bottom of Cadbury Hill. Then Merlin whispered a spell. All at once, the sounds of fighting stilled, and a tide of silvery water rushed over the plain. On its crest came a small boat, empty of any steersman. Coll and Merlin climbed in, and Branwen flew to the masthead.

As the boat turned, Coll saw in front of him the tall green hill of his vision, bathed in the light of the last moon of autumn.

"Avalon, the Isle of Apples," said Merlin gravely. "The resting place of Arthur and his knights. It is time for you to hear the story of how he came here."

✠ 48 ✠

The Isle of Apples

The battle of Camlann was over, and King Arthur lay dying of his wounds. "Take me to the lake," he said to his Companions. "I must keep my promise to the Lady."

A slow, sad procession wound its way through the woods and hills to the silver lake. And there in the mists of evening, Arthur took his sword Caliburn, and with Bedwyr's help, he returned it to the Lady. As it turned over and over in the still, hazy air, a white arm came up out of the water and caught it, and it disappeared.

Then, out of the mists, came a shiver of unearthly music, and a black boat came sailing to shore. It had no oars, nor any rudder, and its one sail was made of spider silk. Four fairy queens sat on its cushions, and as they drew near to Arthur, they beckoned his Companions to carry him to them.

"Farewell, dear friends," he said as the boat turned and glided away. They watched him go with the tears running down their cheeks. Suddenly, the mists parted, and the Companions saw a tall green hill in the distance, covered with apple trees and sunshine. And the trees had blossom and fruit on them at the same time. Then the mists closed again, and the Companions turned and went sadly away.

But King Arthur came safely to Avalon, the fairy isle of apples, and the nine fairy healers who lived on the hill laid him on a golden bed, and healed him. He stayed for a time there, wandering in that magical land where no wind or snow or rain ever come, until his Companions could join him. But what happened then is another story.

The path circled round and round the hill to the very top.

"Where is that door?" muttered Merlin. He took out his staff and thumped it on the ground three times. "Now play your harp, Coll," he shouted as thunder tolled overhead. Coll struck a jangling chord, the earth shifted suddenly, and a long tunnel stretched downwards at their feet.

"Come," said Merlin. "With your help, the spell is broken. I will lead you through the silver gates to where the Treasures are hidden, and tell you the last tale of Arthur as we go."

⌘ 49 ⌘

The Cave of the Sleepers

Merlin rubbed his eyes and groaned. How stiff he was! How long had he been asleep? And what had woken him? He opened his eyes and saw Nimue standing at the cave entrance, shards of crystal sparkling round her feet.

"Awake, Merlin," she said, "and come with me to the Isle of Apples." And she whirled him away on a thundercloud.

There is a place on Avalon where the mists lie thick, even on the sunniest day, and magic runs deeper than buttercup roots. Behind the mists is a cave with a tall silver gate at its entrance, and it was there that Nimue brought Merlin to carry out his greatest task.

Now after all of Arthur's Companions had joined him, they used to ride out among the apple trees on golden horses with manes like winter frost. One evening, as a full moon was rising, they saw an ancient man and a beautiful fairy girl standing under a rowan tree with the mists swirling around them. "Merlin!" cried Arthur, and he galloped his horse forward.

But as he and his twelve Companions reached the mist, Merlin raised Arthur's own harp and played one high, pure note. At once their eyes grew heavy, and they fell forward on their horses' necks in a magical sleep. Nimue opened the silver gate, and Merlin led the horses through into the cave.

Six beds stood down each side of the cave, and one at the head, and in an alcove by each bed rested one of the thirteen treasures of Britain. On each bed Merlin laid one of the Companions, and last of all he laid Arthur down, while Nimue took the thirteen golden horses and whispered spells in their ears till they too lay down at the foot of their masters' beds and fell asleep.

"There they must rest and guard until they are needed once more," whispered Nimue. "And if there is danger, they will ride again to help the land."

Then she and Merlin wove powerful spells around that place, spells of hiding and confusion, till none but the wisest remembered it was there. Merlin sent Arthur's harp up to hang among the summer stars, where it still shines to this day, and then Nimue led him back to the crystal cave.

"Sleep well, dear lord, till the harp calls you back," she said. And the whispering wood rustled in reply.

The warriors lay at rest on their stone beds, their golden horses beside them. In thirteen huge alcoves stood the Treasures.

"But they are all so big," cried Coll. "And it's Wintereve tomorrow. How will I ever get them back to Callanish in time?"

Merlin smiled. "I think you may find the chariot of Morgan the Wealthy useful. It will take you where you need to be swifter than a blowing gale. But there is work to do before you go. I must summon the Hunt," he said, reaching for a small, battered horn hanging on the wall.

The note he blew was lighter than a snowflake's falling, darker than a dragon's heart. It was the sound of starlight and moonshine and sunbeams and all the colours in between. And as it swelled through the cave, there came the sound of hoofbeats from outside.

"The Wild Hunt," breathed Coll, remembering the dark night when Uath had taught him their story.

⌘ 50 ⌘

The Wild Hunt

On Samhain Eve the storms blow in from the farthest west, driving shredded rags of cloud over a yellow full moon. And out of hilltop shadow and shade come King Herla and his ghostly hunters, riding smoke-grey horses of starlight and moonbeams. Through the last sky of autumn they gallop, and before them run the white Wisht Hounds, belling and calling and baying and barking, their red eyes flaming and their red ears a burning beacon in the darkest night places.

Every beast and every bird is hidden, and every door is locked, for those who see the Wild Hunt ride must follow follow follow to the end of earth and beyond.

And the wise ones say that Arthur rides with them, and Finn and Pwyll and Llew, and all the heroes that ever were in this land, or ever will be. Listen! Do you hear them calling?

Coll the Bard Returns

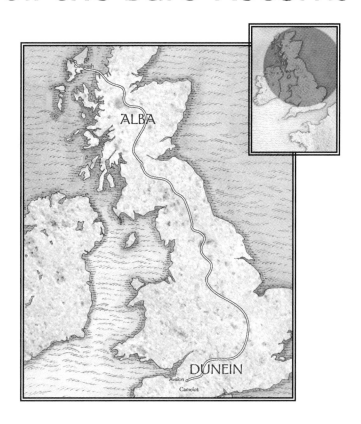

Coll the Bard Returns

The horsemen and their red-eared hounds poured into the cave like smoke and flame, King Herla at their head.

"Awake, Arthur," he cried. "It is time for us to ride! " And as Coll watched, King Arthur and his twelve knights got up from their stone beds and mounted their horses.

Merlin turned to Coll. "Now you must speak," he whispered. Branwen's claws dug into his shoulder as Coll stepped forward into the milling mass of dogs and horses. His dream finally made sense, and he knew just what he had to do.

"Your majesties," he called. "The magic is weak now in Avalon, and the magic Treasures of Britain are in danger from raiders from oversea. The spirits of the Otherworld have called me to take the Treasures to a safer place, but I cannot fight the raiders as well. Will you save the land from this danger?"

"We will," said the deep voices of King Arthur and King Herla. And together they and their hero warriors rode out of the cave to battle the raiders and drive them away, back to their longships and far away over the sea. Then Coll drew the magic chariot of Morgan the Wealthy from its alcove and loaded the rest of the Treasures into it. They fitted easily, as Merlin had known they would.

"Will you come with me?" he asked Merlin.

Merlin shook his head. "I shall go back to the twisted wood and prepare a place for Arthur and I to sleep again. This time no one will wake either of us until the last days of Britain come, and that is in a time so far off that it can't be imagined."

So Coll climbed into the chariot with Branwen.

"Take us to Callanish," he said. And at once the chariot rose into the air, and swept over the Island of Britain so fast that as dusk fell on Wintereve, and the waning autumn moon rose in the sky, Coll saw Callanish beneath him.

The torches flamed around the circle as the procession of druids wove its way around the tall stones in the Wintereve ceremony that welcomed the ending of the year. The chariot of Morgan the Wealthy swept down from a sky full of stars and landed in front of Ollach, Uath and Fergal.

"I'm back," said Coll the Bard.
"Cark!" said Branwen the Raven. "Me too."

Lucy Coats has been fascinated by myths and legends for as long as she can remember. She worked as an editor in children's publishing and now writes full time. She lives in Northamptonshire with her husband, two children and pets.

Anthony Lewis has illustrated over two hundred children's books since graduating from the Liverpool School of Art with first-class honours. He is married with three children and lives in rural Cheshire.

ATTICUS THE STORYTELLER'S 100 GREEK MYTHS

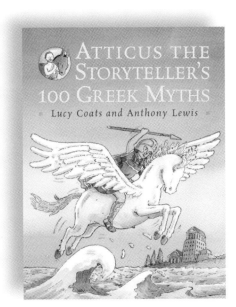

Long ago, in ancient Greece, gods and goddesses, heroes and heroines lived together with fearful monsters and every kind of fabulous beast that ever flew or walked or swam ... Atticus the Storyteller leaves his family in Crete and sets off on a year-long journey round Greece with his donkey, Melissa, to take part in the great Storytelling Festival near Troy. Wherever he goes he tells stories to anyone who will listen – sailors, shepherds, actors, athletes, and children. The tales he tells are linked by the story of his journey through the ancient sites where the stories originally happened.

'For a very long time there has been a real lack of a superb retelling of the Greek myths for younger children. This version will be with us for a long time ... as it is vibrant, immediate and above all, fun! A really lovely book for all the family to share.'
BOOKS FOR KEEPS

FIFTY OF THE WONDERFUL TALES FROM
ATTICUS THE STORYTELLER'S 100 GREEK MYTHS
ARE GATHERED TOGETHER IN ...

THE BOY WHO FELL
FROM THE SKY

Theseus and the Minotaur, Daedalus and Icarus, Persephone in the Underworld, Perseus and the Gorgon, King Midas and the Asses' Ears, the twelve labours of Heracles are some of the all-time favourites in this wonderful book.

A SECOND SELECTION OF VIBRANT RETELLINGS, TAKEN
FROM ATTICUS THE STORYTELLER'S 100 GREEK MYTHS ...

THE WOODEN HORSE

This superb collection includes the well-loved tales of Echo and Narcissus, Orpheus and Eurydice, the Trojan horse, Arachne the weaver, Phaëthon and the sun chariot, and the wanderings of Odysseus, who encounters the Cyclops, the Sirens, and other memorable figures.